Lauren   Mackay

STACEY AND THE MISSING RING

"Claud, I know what you're doing," I said. My stomach was in a knot. "You're looking for that ring, aren't you?"

Claudia didn't answer straight away, but at least she took her hand out of the box for a moment. Then she drew in a deep breath.

"Well, I am looking for it," she admitted. "I started to think on my way over here. You know, you did talk a lot about wanting a diamond ring. And now one is missing. I was wondering if this really was such a coincidence, after all."

"How *could* you?" I cried. "I thought you were my best friend." I felt as if I might start to cry any minute, but I fought back my tears.

"I just thought that before this went any further, I'd better make sure you really didn't have the ring," said Claudia.

"And?" I asked. "Are you sure now that you've gone through all my private belongings?" I felt less like crying then. I was starting to get angry . . .

STACEY AND THE
MISSING RING

Ann M. Martin

Scholastic Children's Books,
Scholastic Publications Ltd,
7-9 Pratt Street, London NW1 0AE

Sholastic Inc.,
555 Broadway, New York, NY 10012-3999,USA

Scholastic Canada Ltd,
123 Newkirk Road, Richmond Hill,
Ontario L4C 3G5, Canada

Ashton Scholastic Pty Ltd,
P O Box 579, Gosford, New South Wales,
Australia

Ashton Scholastic Ltd,
Private Bag 1, Penrose, Auckland,
New Zealand

First published in the US by Scholastic Inc., 1991
First published in the UK by Scholastic Publications Ltd, 1994

ISBN 0 590 55300 3

Typeset in Plantin by Contour Typesetters, Southall, London
Printed by Cox & Wyman Ltd, Reading, Berks.

10 9 8 7 6 5 4 3 2 1

*The author gratefully acknowledges
Ellen Miles
for her help in
preparing this manuscript.*

1st CHAPTER

Please don't tell any of my friends. They'd think I was nuts if they knew. But it's true. Sometimes I actually like doing housework.

Maybe you know what I mean. There can be something really satisfying about taking that last swipe with a mop, or polishing a tap until it shines, or looking at a newly cleaned window with the sun sparkling through it.

Or maybe you just think I'm nuts.

Anyway, whether you agree with me or not, you'll have to take my word for it. I was having a good time that Saturday morning, helping my mother with the housework. Cleaning wasn't all we'd done, though.

First, we'd made breakfast—or rather, my mum made breakfast, and I ate it. She cooked my favourite: blueberry pancakes. I love them because they are naturally sweet, so I don't miss the oceans of maple syrup that most people drown their pancakes in.

I can't have maple syrup on my pancakes because I've got diabetes.

That's right. I, Stacey McGill, thirteen-year-old eighth-grader, am a diabetic. In case you don't know what that means, let me explain. First of all, it's a disease I'll have for the rest of my life, so I've had to learn to live with it. My pancreas (that's one of those weird-shaped organs inside you) doesn't do its job properly. It doesn't make this stuff called insulin, which people need to help them digest carbohydrates and sugar.

Since my body can't deal with sugar very well, I have to be very, very careful about what I eat and when I eat it. Also, I have to supply the insulin that my pancreas can't. How do I do that? Well, I give myself injections every day. I know, ugh-ugh-ugh, right? But it's not so bad once you get used to it.

And I don't have much choice, anyway. If I don't look after myself, I can get *really* ill. In fact, not all that long ago, I found that out for certain. I slipped up a little with my diet and stopped taking care of myself the way I should, and guess what? I ended up in hospital. I don't want that to happen again if I can help it, so I'm back to being Little Miss Healthy of Stoneybrook, Connecticut.

Stoneybrook's the town where my mum and I live. We didn't always live here, though. I grew up in New York City—and boy, did I love that city. I used to be a real New Yorker—I loved shopping at Bloomingdale's, going to the Hard Rock Cafe, seeing musicals on Broadway. But you know what? Now I love Stoneybrook, too.

My family first moved from New York to Stoneybrook a while back, when my dad got transferred by his company. We adjusted pretty well to the move—in fact, I was really, really happy in Stoneybrook. Not very long after we'd moved there, I became a member of this great club—a babysitting club. I'd always loved babysitting, and joining the club was like getting a whole group of best friends all at once.

But the club's another story. I'll tell you more about that later. I'm just trying to explain why I was so happy in Stoney- brook—so that you'll understand what a shock it was when my dad got transferred *back* to the city and we had to leave!

Guess what? Once we were back in New York, my parents started to argue a lot, and before long they'd decided to get a divorce. Then my dad decided to get a little flat on the East Side of Manhattan, and my mum decided to move back to Stoneybrook, where she'd been happy. It was up to me to choose where I wanted to live.

I hope you never have to make a decision like that.

It wasn't easy, but finally I realized that I

would be happiest living with my mum in Stoneybrook. I do visit my dad fairly often, and I love being in New York during those weekends, but you know what? I think I made the right decision. It's tough being a "divorced kid" (I'm still trying to work it all out), but here in Stoneybrook I have a lot of good friends to help me through it.

Also, I've got pretty close to my mum, and I think we make a good team. Like on that Saturday morning. She would dust the furniture, and I would polish it. She would sweep the floor, and I would mop it. We were working well together.

Mum had tuned the radio to an oldies station, and we were having a great time singing along to these songs that had been popular when she was a teenager. Over the years she's taught me the words to a lot of them, so now I can "Do the Twist" and "Shake it up, Baby" with the best of them.

I'd just been dancing with the mop to "I Wanna Hold Your Hand", when the song ended and Roy Orbison came on singing "Pretty Woman". My mum wandered into the kitchen with a faraway look in her eyes. "I love that song," she said. "It always reminds me of my sixteenth birthday."

It's hard to imagine your mother as a sixteen-year-old.

"Did you have a sweet-sixteen party?" I asked.

"Are you kidding? I had the biggest, best

4

sweet-sixteen party of the decade. Didn't I ever show you the photos?" She dragged me into the living room and sat me on the sofa. Then she pulled an old, battered photo album off the shelf.

"Oh, right," I said, as soon as I saw the pictures. "Now I remember. That's where you were wearing that funny dress, and you had that weird hairdo—what's it called? A wasps' nest?"

"A beehive," she said, laughing. "And I don't think my dress was that funny. It was my first real grown-up dress, and I had high heels to match. I felt like a million dollars that day."

We looked at the photographs together. "You do look happy," I said.

"I always loved celebrating my birthday," Mum told me. "And that one was the best fun of all."

"I love my birthday, too." I said. Then I remembered something I'd been meaning to bring up. "In fact," I added in a rush, deciding that now was as good a time as any, "since my birthday has always had such a special meaning for me, I was wondering if you might like to help me buy this ring I saw at the Stoneybrook Jewellers'." There. I'd said it.

"Ring?" asked my mother. "What does this have to do with your birthday? Your birthday is months away." She closed the photo album and looked at me.

"I know," I said. "And I didn't mean that the ring would be a birthday present. See, it's a birthstone ring. It's gorgeous, and it would be so—so *meaningful* for me." I looked at her hopefully. "I just thought that maybe you could help me pay for it."

Actually I had hoped that she would *buy* it for me, but I was already getting the feeling that there was no way *that* was going to happen.

"What is your birthstone, Stacey?" Mum asked. She wasn't making any offers, I noticed.

"Well," I answered. "It's—it's a diamond." Somehow I knew she wasn't going to be thrilled with that news.

"Diamond, hmm?" she said. "I'm not sure a diamond ring is appropriate for a girl your age." She frowned.

"Lots of girls have birthstone rings!" I said. Actually, I only knew two girls who had them, and neither of their birthstones was a diamond. I think one was an amethyst and one was a garnet. I was pretty sure that neither cost quite as much as a diamond. But I kept that to myself.

"Lots of girls . . ." said my mother. "Well. How much does the ring cost?"

Suddenly I wondered if I'd picked the right time for this after all. Mum and I had been having such a nice time together, and now things were about to turn sour. Even so, I gritted my teeth and told her how much the ring cost.

I thought my mum was going to faint.

"Anastasia Elizabeth McGill!" she said. "You *have* to be kidding. Don't you think that's a little *extravagant*?"

"I—I just thought that we might be able to afford—" I started to say.

"Afford a diamond ring?" she interrupted. "It seems to me that there are plenty of better ways for us to spend money."

Uh-oh. This wasn't going in the right direction at all.

"Now, I might be willing to give you ten dollars towards the ring," Mum went on, "but that's it. I certainly can't—and won't—*buy* it for you."

Ten dollars! Ten dollars wouldn't go far towards that ring. I'd have to babysit every day for the rest of my life to make up the difference. All of a sudden I got angry. I don't ask my mum for much, and now she was acting as if I were being outrageous.

"Dad would buy it for me," I muttered.

"What?" she asked. "Did you say what I think you said?"

"Dad would buy it for me," I repeated more loudly. So what if she was cross. I was, too.

"You know," she said, a bit sadly, "you may be right about that."

For a moment I felt guilty. "I know you

don't earn as much money as Dad does," I said. "But—"

"There's no but about it, Stacey," she said. "I *don't* earn as much as he does, and money is always going to be tighter in Stoneybrook than it is in New York. You can't have everything you want."

"But I don't ask for everything!" I said. "It's just this one ring."

But my mum wasn't even listening. She was off on another track by then. "You know, Stacey, ever since you were ill, your father and I have been trying hard not to put you in the middle of our arguments," she said.

"I know," I answered. "And I appreciate it." (Sometimes I used to feel like a Ping-Pong ball being batted around, but when I was really ill, I had a talk with my parents, and they'd promised to change.)

"And I've been trying to make sure that I don't ask you for too much information about your father," Mum continued. She used to pump me all the time about what we did and where we went. I was glad she'd stopped. "But," Mum continued, "I can't help noticing that you come home with all kinds of nice things every time you visit him. He's treating you like a princess when you're in New York, and I don't think it's good for you."

"But he's not, really!" I said. It was true that when the divorce first happened, Dad

8

sometimes bought me incredibly expensive stuff, trying to make up for all the pain he thought he'd put me through. But now he knew that I didn't need—or want—him to do that. He still bought me presents, I'll admit, but small things, mostly.

Actually, I wasn't sure Dad *would* buy me that ring. The "old" dad might have, but we've got past that stage now. He'd probably just give me a hard time about it, like Mum.

Mum looked at me doubtfully. "Well, whether he's still spoiling you or not, the answer remains the same for me. I will not buy you that ring."

"Fine!" I said. "That's just *fine*." I jumped up from the sofa. "Who cares about a stupid old ring, anyway?" Now *I* was upset. "Have we finished cleaning?" I asked.

"I can do the rest, I suppose," Mum answered. "Why? Did you have any plans?"

"I didn't," I answered. "But I'm about to make some."

That pleasant Saturday morning had turned into a total drag. Suddenly I needed to get away from my mum for a while. I headed for the phone to call my friends and see if anybody wanted to go shopping.

2nd CHAPTER

I decided to phone Kristy first. If she wanted to go shopping, there was a good chance that she could talk her brother Charlie into driving us to the shopping arcade.

Kristy Thomas is the chairman of that club I was telling you about, the Babysitters Club. She's a good friend; in fact, all the members are my good friends. That's one of the reasons I love the club so much.

As I dialled Kristy's number, I tried to guess who would answer the phone at her house. I often do that when I phone her, just because it's a challenging game; the phone could get picked up by any one of about twenty people.

Well, maybe not quite twenty. But Kristy does have a big—and interesting—family.

First there's her mum, who was divorced just like my mum. Only her divorce happened a long time ago, when Kristy's dad up and left the family. At that point, the "family" was Kristy and her older brothers, Sam and Charlie, as well as her little brother, David Michael, who was just a baby at the time. (To keep you up to date, David Michael's seven now, Sam is fifteen, and Charlie is seventeen.)

Mrs Thomas did a great job of holding her family together after Mr Thomas left— and it wasn't always easy. Then, not long ago, she met Watson Brewer and ended up getting married again.

Who's Watson Brewer? Well, he's a real *millionaire*—and also a pretty nice person. Kristy was lucky to get him for a stepfather. And along with Watson, she got a couple of stepsiblings: Karen, who's just turned seven, and Andrew, who's four. They live with their mum (Watson's ex-wife) most of the time, but Kristy loves the time they spend with their father—every other weekend and certain holidays. Karen and Andrew are great kids.

When Mrs Thomas and Watson got married, the family became so big that it made sense for them to move into Watson's mansion—that's right, I said *mansion*—on the other side of town. But I suppose that once they got into the mansion, Watson and Kristy's mum decided that there was too much space left over and they needed to make the family even *bigger*.

That's when they adopted a little Vietnamese girl they named Emily Michelle. She is *the* cutest two-year-old you've ever seen. Soon after she arrived, Watson and Kristy's mum realized they'd need help looking after her, so they invited Kristy's grandmother, Nannie, to come and live with them too. Phew! I suppose it's a full house—or mansion—now. Especially when you take Boo-Boo (that's Watson's mean old cat) and Shannon (David Michael's puppy) into account.

Anyway, this time when I phoned Kristy's, guess who answered! Kristy herself, for once. She thought the shopping arcade was a great idea, and she told me to phone everybody else while she talked Charlie into giving us a ride.

It might sound as if Kristy was being a little bossy, and maybe she was. But that's just the way she is. Kristy is what teachers call a "good leader". She's always having great ideas, and she knows how to get people to help her put them into action. She's a bit like a grown-up in that way, although it's funny because in other ways she can be immature.

She doesn't care much about make-up or boys or that kind of stuff, and she still dresses like a kid: jeans, polonecks, trainers. She doesn't play around with her hair, either. Kristy is pretty short—in fact, she's the shortest girl in our class—so she even looks younger than the rest of us. And I suppose you'd call her a tomboy. For example, she coaches a softball team made up of little kids. That's Kristy.

I decided to follow her "orders" and call the others, starting with my best friend Claudia. Claudia Kishi is the coolest dresser and most exotic-looking girl in the eighth grade. She's exotic-looking because she's Japanese-American, with brown almond-shaped eyes, a gorgeous complexion, and long, thick black hair. She's the coolest dresser because she's not afraid to try out new things, and because she is so creative.

Claudia's an artist—she can draw, paint, make sculptures, and do any other kind of art better than anyone I know. She spends a lot of her time and energy on her art, a lot more than she does on her schoolwork, that's for sure. Claud isn't much of an intellectual. Not that she isn't clever. She *is* clever, even though she isn't a certified genius like her older sister Janine. Claud just doesn't care as much about schoolwork as she does about art.

Claud has a couple of other passions, ones that her parents don't encourage as much as her artwork. One is Nancy Drew books: she loves reading them even though her parents think they're rubbish. The other is junk food, which she can't get enough of. She hides her mysteries and her crisps, Kit-Kats, and Mars Bars all over her room.

Claudia was *definitely* up for going to the arcade. Next, I called Mary Anne and Dawn.

Mary Anne Spier looks like the "girl next door". She's got brown hair and brown eyes, just like Kristy, and although she has some cool clothes, she's still a pretty conservative dresser. Mary Anne just looks *sweet*—and she is. She's sensitive, and caring, and a really loyal friend. (Such a good friend that she manages to be *best* friends with two people at once: Kristy and Dawn Schafer.)

Mary Anne's mum died when Mary Anne was really young, so her dad was left to bring her up. Mr Spier used to be incredibly strict about what Mary Anne could do, and what she could wear. He even had rules about how she could wear her hair. (And I'm not talking about Mary Anne wanting a Mohican or pink hair. She had to struggle for years just to get her hair out of plaits.)

Mr Spier has finally relaxed, though. He let Mary Anne change her hair and her clothes, allowed her to get a kitten (a grey one, called Tigger), and eased up on the rules and regulations.

I think that when Mr Spier loosened up, he also realized he was ready for some changes in his own life. Like falling in love and getting married! Mr Spier got married again to his old high-school sweetheart, who just happened to be the mother of Dawn Schafer, another club member and, as I've mentioned before, one of Mary Anne's two best friends.

Here's how it happened: Dawn's mother grew up in Stoneybrook, but then she moved to California, got married, and had two kids (Dawn and her younger brother Jeff, who's now ten). When she got divorced, she moved back to Stoneybrook with Dawn and Jeff. Dawn and Mary Anne became friends at school, and discovered—by looking through old high-school yearbooks—that their parents had once dated! And when Mrs Schafer and Mr Spier got together again, the rest was history. Now Mary Anne and her father and Tigger live with Dawn and her mum in an old, old farmhouse that's big enough for all of them. Dawn's brother Jeff doesn't live there, because it turned out he missed California and his dad so much that he was miserable in Stoneybrook. So Jeff moved back to California to live with his father.

Dawn, our California girl, has long, pale blonde hair, blue eyes, and a great sense of style that lets her look very casual and very cool all at once. Dawn is her own person, and she goes her own way, not caring much what other people think of her. I admire her for that.

The main thing Dawn likes about Stoneybrook (besides the Babysitters Club which we invited her to join) is that she can get tofu here. It's a staple of her incredibly healthy diet. And the main thing she dislikes about it is—guess what—*winter*. Dawn's never become convinced that ice-skating and snowball fights fall under the classification of "fun". Beaches are fun. Roller-skating on a boardwalk is fun. But anything you do in below-freezing weather, according to Dawn, cannot be fun.

Mary Anne answered the phone at their house and said she would love to go to the arcade. She wanted to stop at the pet shop and buy a new toy for Tigger. (Boy, is that kitten spoiled.) Dawn wanted to go, too, even though she didn't really have anything she needed to shop for.

My next call was to Mallory Pike, one of the two younger members of the club. (The other one is Jessica Ramsey.) Mallory may be younger than the rest of us (she and Jessi are eleven and in the sixth grade), but she's really pretty mature. I think she's had to grow up fast because she's the oldest in a *huge* family. Early on, her parents needed her help with the younger kids. All seven of them!

Mal has *seven* younger brothers and sisters, ranging in age from ten (those are

16

the triplets: Adam, Byron and Jordan) down to five (that's Claire). In between, there's Vanessa (she's nine), Nicky (eight), and Margo (seven). So Mal's been baby-sitting for a long, long time.

The frustrating thing for Mallory these days is that even though her parents give her a lot of responsibility, they aren't quite ready to let her grow up. Mal would like to get contact lenses instead of having to wear glasses, and she would like to wear her red hair in a trendier style, and dress in wilder clothes. But so far, the most her parents have let her do is get her ears pierced. They say the rest will have to wait until she's older, so Mal just has to be patient.

While she's waiting, Mal entertains herself with fantasies of becoming a children's book author/illustrator. She loves writing and drawing, and she's good at both things, so don't be surprised if you see her name on a book jacket one day. Mal also has fantasies of being a horse owner. She loves reading, and horse stories are her favourites. But the Pikes' house is much too crowded for the golden palomino Mal dreams of.

Mallory's best friend, Jessica Ramsey, loves horse books, too. In fact, when I phoned Mallory, Jessi was over there, sitting in Mal's room reading *Black Beauty* for the thousandth time. Mal was reading

17

one of the Misty books. They both decided to leave the books for a while, though, and join us at the arcade.

Jessi's family is different from Mallory's. She's only got one sister (Becca, who's nine) and one brother (Squirt—that's his nickname—who's just a baby). The Ramseys are different in another way, too. They're black. Of course, that isn't a problem for Mal, or for any of us club members, but some people in the neighbourhood weren't all that happy when the Ramseys moved in. By now things have got better, but they weren't easy at the beginning.

What does Jessi fantasize about? (Besides being thirteen, that is.) Jessi dreams of being a ballerina one day. I'd have to say that her dream is pretty close to reality, too. Jessi's already one of the best dancers in her ballet school in Stamford. She's got the lead in more than one major production, and she's really something to see when she's on stage. Jessi is *talented* and she works really hard at her dancing. That's why I think she'll be taking curtain calls in a big New York City theatre one day in the future.

I put the phone down, now that I'd finished with my calls, and went into my bedroom to change and get ready for shopping. My mum was still vacuuming downstairs, and I wondered if I should make up with her before I left. But then I heard Charlie honk his car horn outside, and I looked out of the window to see Kristy motioning to me to hurry. So instead of making up, I just told my mum where I was going and gave her a wave as I ran out of the house. I was really looking forward to spending the day at the arcade with my friends.

3rd CHAPTER

"Hey, everybody," I said, as I climbed into the back seat. "Thank you for driving us, Charlie."

"No big deal," he answered. "I was going to the arcade anyway to see a film with some of the guys."

"And to check out the girls, too," said Kristy. "Right?"

Charlie went red. I thought perhaps I should change the subject. "Isn't the Junk Bucket running?" I asked him. The Junk Bucket is Charlie's car, and it's a pretty good name for the clattery old thing. But that day, Charlie wasn't driving his car. We were riding along in true luxury, in Watson's estate car.

"It's running," he said. "But barely. Watson said I could take his car today since he wasn't using it."

We stopped to pick up Dawn and Mary

Anne, and they squeezed in next to me. "Mmmm," I said. "Somebody smells good. What is that smell?"

"Must be my new shampoo," answered Dawn. "It's called 'Wildflower Wash'." She tossed her hair, and I could smell the sweet scent again.

Charlie coughed. "Smells more like 'Accident in the Perfume Factory' to me," he said. We all cracked up.

Jessi and Mal were waiting at the Pikes' house, sitting on the porch with the triplets. "Can't we go, too?" pleaded Byron.

"Sorry," said Jessi. "Girls only."

"But Charlie's a boy," said Adam.

"Girls and *grown-up* boys only," said Mal. "Sorry, boys. Maybe another time."

"That's what you always say," muttered Jordan.

Mal and Jessi waved at the boys and ran to the car. Since it was getting pretty crowded, they decided to curl up in the very back. They looked like a couple of little kids there, giggling as they wiggled into comfortable positions.

The last stop was at Claudia's. She ran out as soon as we honked, dressed in her current favourite outfit. Claud looked terrific in black leggings, red high-top trainers, and an oversized red sweater. She was carrying a red plastic lunch box as a bag. Claudia jumped into the front seat with Kristy, and we were on our way.

When we pulled into the shopping centre's car park, we couldn't see any empty spaces. Charlie groaned. "Seems as if this is the place to be today," he said, as he drove up and down the lanes. "Oh, here's one," he said finally.

"Charlie," said Kristy, once he'd pulled into the space. "We must be about two miles away from the arcade. I can hardly see Sears from here!"

"I told you I'd get you here, and I did," Charlie answered. "Want me to call you a taxi to take you the rest of the way?"

"Oh, ha, ha," said Kristy. "No, thanks. I think we'll be able to walk it in an hour or two."

"Good," said Charlie. "Listen, I've gotta go. I'm supposed to meet the guys in five minutes. How about if we meet at Mr Pretzel at four o'clock?"

We agreed that that sounded fine. "Bye, Charlie," called Kristy. "And thanks!" Charlie ran across the car park. "I bet it's not 'the guys' he's meeting," said Kristy. "He seems to be in a real hurry, if you know what I mean." We all giggled.

When we pushed open the doors of the arcade, I stood for a minute and took a deep breath. I love the way the arcade smells—like new shoes and cookies baking and pizza hot out of the oven and perfume and, well, just a lot of good smells mixed together.

The place was packed. Groups of kids were hanging around on every corner. Mothers and fathers pushed buggies and dragged whining toddlers from shop to shop. Couples walked along holding hands, smiling at each other as if nobody else existed.

In the shop windows were bright signs, and mannequins dressed in really cool (and probably very expensive) clothes. Silver balloons floated from stalls in the middle of the main walkway. Music blared from the record store. The fountain in the centre of the arcade shot a spray of pink water high into the air.

I love the arcade.

We sat down on the edge of the fountain, which is one of the cool places to hang out, and started to plan our afternoon. Mary Anne couldn't wait to go to the pet shop, and Jessi and Mal said they'd go there, too.

"I love looking at the puppies," said Mal.

"I know," said Jessi with a sigh. "Except I always feel so bad that I can't take them home with me. They look so sad in their little cages."

Claudia said she'd pass on looking at the animals. "I want to check out this new line of trainers I saw in a magazine," she said. "They look pretty outrageous."

"Sounds good to me," I said. "I don't

23

have much money to spend, but I'm always up for looking at shoes."

Dawn wanted to window-shop, too, but Kristy voted to stick with Mary Anne. So we ended up splitting into two groups, and we agreed to meet at the pet shop in an hour.

"Before we do anything else," said Claudia as soon as we were on our way, "we've *got* to stop for nachos. I'm starving."

I wasn't interested in nachos (I have to be really careful about what kind of junk food I eat), but I didn't mind stopping at the Tortilla Queen place, and neither did Dawn. A really cute guy works there. . . .

But it must have been his day off. There was no sign of him at the counter, just this greasy-looking bald man who looked incredibly bored. We sat by the window while Claud ate her nachos, watching the crowds go by. I love looking at what people are wearing at the arcade—everything from ripped jeans to fur coats.

"Okay," said Claud, wiping her fingers with a serviette. "Now where should we go?"

We walked slowly down one side of the arcade, stopping in whatever shops looked like fun. Dawn loves the T-shirt shop, so we spent some time in there. She tried to decide between a blue shirt with a picture of whales on it and a yellow one that said "Go For It" in big black letters, but finally ended up getting neither. "I don't really *need* a new T-shirt right now," she said.

"I don't really *need* new trainers, either," said Claud. "But that's not going to stop me!" She led the way to the shoe shop. Claud has got the biggest trainer collection of anyone I know, honestly. She's got red ones (two other pairs besides the ones she was wearing that day) and purple, black, white and polka-dotted ones. I bet she could wear a different pair of trainers for every day of the month.

"What do you think?" she asked, holding up a pair of lace-and-sequin-trimmed pink high-tops. "Pretty cool, right?"

I knew from looking through that month's magazines that those shoes were past cool. "Nice," I said. "Can you afford them?"

"Yup. I don't need any new art materials at the moment, and I'm sure I'll be babysitting a lot this month, so there's no need to save the money I've got." She asked the assistant for a size six, and tried them on. "I love them," she told him, as she checked herself in the mirror.

While Claudia was paying for the trainers, Dawn and I watched two women try on high heels. The funny thing was that both of them pretended they had the tiniest, most delicate feet. They started out asking the assistant for "size five, please," but they ended up working their way to "size eight and a half, I suppose" before they could squeeze their feet into the shoes.

Dawn and I were nearly dying with held-in laughter by the time we made it out of the store. We exploded as soon as we'd got through the door. "'Oh, well, size eleven ought to do it,'" said Dawn, imitating one woman. "'But I'm a *small* size eleven, mind you.'"

Tears were running down my cheeks from laughing so much. We walked past a few more shops, laughing again every time we thought about the women, and then we reached the pet shop.

Mary Anne had bought a toy mouse for Tigger. When we arrived, she and the others were gazing lovingly at the puppies and kittens that were for sale.

"Isn't he *adorable*?" asked Jessi, pointing to a black Labrador retriever puppy. He was a pretty cute dog, I had to admit.

"Look at this one," said Kristy, dragging me over to see a bulldog puppy in another cage. "Isn't he something?"

"He's something, all right," I answered. "If you happen to like squashed faces!"

After the pet shop, we went to Friendly's for ice cream. At least, the others had ice cream. I ate a tuna fish sandwich, and it tasted great. I wasn't even envious of Claud's Hot Fudge Brownie Delite. Well, not *too* envious, anyway.

We didn't have to meet Charlie for

another half hour, so after Friendly's, we decided to cruise up the other side of the arcade. As we were walking, I spotted something in the window of Town and Country Jewellery. A birthstone ring display! I came to a complete stop and looked closer, the others crowding behind me. The diamond ring was beautiful—a circle of diamonds in a gold setting—but it cost a *lot* more than the other one I'd seen.

I told everybody how much I wanted a ring like that, and about the fight I'd had that morning with my mum. Claud bent closer to look at the price of the ring. "Wow!" she said. "I've never had a piece of jewellery that cost anything like that."

"I wouldn't *dare* to ask my parents for a diamond ring," said Mallory. "Even if it was my birthstone."

"But it *is* totally gorgeous, don't you think?" I asked.

Everybody nodded, but they looked a bit overwhelmed. I wished they could have been more on my side. I wanted Claud to say, "You deserve a ring like that, Stacey, and your mother's a meanie not to buy it for you." But she didn't say that.

Still, when I got home that night, I couldn't resist bringing up the subject again with my mother. She seemed to be in a good mood—she'd forgotten our argument, obviously—so I decided to go for it. I described the ring I'd seen that day, and then I told her how much it cost. "So the one at Stoneybrook Jewellers is really a bargain in comparison," I said thinking that she'd be convinced by my logical argument.

"Stacey," she replied, "you don't seem to understand. The answer is no. Absolutely not. I am *not* buying a diamond ring for you."

What could I say? Nothing. Instead, I headed upstairs to call Claudia and complain about my hard-hearted mother.

4th CHAPTER

By Monday afternoon, when I went to Claud's house for our club meeting, I was feeling a bit better. I'd decided to forget about the ring, since it seemed that I wasn't going to get it. My mum had made her feelings clear, and you know what? I didn't even want to ask my dad. It's true that he sometimes spoils me. Then my mum gets angry, and I feel in the middle again. Who needs that?

I reached Claud's room early, and she and Kristy were the only ones there so far. Claud was there because we meet in her room, and Kristy was there because Kristy likes to be punctual. Kristy was sitting where she usually sits. In the director's chair. She was wearing her visor, and she'd stuck a pencil behind one ear. Ready for action.

Claud was sitting cross-legged on her

bed, a sketch pad balanced on her knees. She was looking up at Kristy and then down at the paper. Her charcoal made quick scratchy lines. Then she rubbed the paper to blend them in. I sat next to her on the bed and looked at the drawing. "Hey, that's really good!" I said. I don't know why I was surprised. I know my best friend is a great artist. But this picture just looked so—so *Kristyish*. I couldn't even put my finger on why it looked so much like her. Was it her nose? Her hair? The way she was leaning in the chair? I don't know. It was just Kristy, there on the paper.

"Almost time to start," said Kristy, as Mary Anne and Dawn walked in. They plopped down on the bed, too.

"Great picture!" said Dawn.

"Thanks," replied Claud. "But look at these hands. I'd better go and wash them." She held out her hands to show us how filthy they were. They were smudged and blackened with charcoal.

As soon as Claud had left the room, Kristy grabbed the sketch. "This really looks like me?" she asked. We nodded. She studied the drawing closely. When Claud came back in, Kristy asked if she could keep the picture.

"Of course," said Claudia. "It's yours."

Mallory walked in just then, with Jessi right behind her. They took their usual places on the floor. Kristy passed the picture to them. "That's great!" said Mal. "Would you do me some time?"

At that moment, I saw the digital clock on Claud's night table flip to 5:30. "Order!" said Kristy. "Time for the meeting."

As I said, Kristy likes to be punctual.

Actually, I think it's a good thing that she is so serious about running our club occasionally. That way it's more like a business than a club. We have fun, but we also get the job done.

Kristy opens the meetings because she's the chairman. And she's the chairman because starting the club was her idea. None of us had thought of a babysitters club before Kristy. She's good at coming up with new ideas—ideas that really work.

Kristy got the idea for the club back in the seventh grade. That was before her mum married Watson, so Kristy still lived on Bradford Court, right opposite Claudia. Anyway, Kristy used to babysit for her little brother, David Michael, after school, and also whenever her mum wanted to go out in the evening. If Kristy had other plans, Charlie or Sam would take over.

But one night, everybody was busy and Mrs Thomas decided she'd have to phone a sitter. She was on the phone for about an hour, calling everybody she could think of, but nobody could take the job. She was getting more and more frustrated, but

Kristy, watching her, was becoming excited.

She'd had an idea.

What if her mum could make one phone call that would put her in touch with a whole group of experienced sitters? This would have saved her a lot of time and energy, and she would have been guaranteed a sitter. The next day Kristy told Claudia and Mary Anne about her idea, and they saw straight away how well it could work. But they thought that three girls weren't enough, so Claud suggested inviting me to join, too. (My family had just moved to Stoneybrook, and Claud and I had started to become friends.) Then when Dawn moved to Stoneybrook, she joined, too.

The club worked perfectly from the beginning. We've always met in Claud's room, between 5:30 and 6:00 every Monday, Wednesday, and Friday. Why Claud's room? Because she has her very own phone, with a private line. By using her number for our club, we avoid tying up any adults' phones. Since we use her room and her phone, Claud was made vice chairman.

Anyway, while we're meeting, parents can phone and arrange for whatever sitting jobs they need. How do they know to call? Well, by now our business is mostly advertised by word of mouth—parents telling other parents—but at first we got the word out by distributing leaflets. Once in a while we still hand them out if we feel we need extra business. The leaflets explain about the club and tell parents when and where to call.

You might be wondering when Jessi and Mal joined the club. Well, that was during the time my family left Stoneybrook to move back to New York. The club had so much business that my friends decided they needed more members, and Jessi and Mal were perfect candidates. Luckily, when I returned to Stoneybrook, there was no question that I would be able to join again, too.

What's my job in the club? I'm the treasurer. That means I keep track of how much money we earn. We each get to keep whatever money we make, but it's interesting to know the total amount. I also get to collect subs, which I was about to do that very minute.

"It's Monday," I said, when Kristy asked whether there was any club business. "You all know what *that* means!" I had a big smile on my face but everybody else was frowning. They hate parting with their money but I just love collecting it. I like to keep our manila envelope fat with money in case of an emergency.

Of course, we don't often have emergencies, so the money is spent on other things. Like paying Charlie to drive Kristy to meetings, now that she no longer lives across the street from "headquarters". And for pizza parties or sleepover snacks. And for—

"Stacey," said Dawn suddenly. I realized I'd been daydreaming. "I need some new markers for my Kid-Kit. Is there enough money?"

Kid-Kits. That's just what I was going to tell you about. Kid-Kits are boxes that we've decorated to look cool. Inside, we put books and crayons and stickers and toys that kids love. The kits were another of Kristy's ideas when she noticed that kids always seem to like *other* kid's toys better than their own. Most of the stuff in our kits isn't new, but it is different. The kits help to make us popular sitters!

I counted out some money and handed it to Dawn. "Is that enough?" I asked.

"Certainly," she said. "If I want to buy two markers!" She made a face at me. "Come on, Stacey. You can spare a little more."

I dug out two more dollars. "Okay?" I said. Dawn nodded. I heard some giggling, but I ignored it. Everybody thinks I'm stingy, but I'm just protecting *their* better interests. If I didn't watch every penny, there wouldn't be money in the treasury when we need it.

"Jessi," said Kristy just then, "I noticed that you didn't write up your last job in the club notebook."

"Oh, that's right. I'm sorry," said Jessi.

"I didn't have time because I had an extra dance class this week. I'll do it right now." She reached for the book.

The club notebook is where we record all the jobs we go on each week. Once again, this was Kristy's idea—and it's not one of her more popular ones. It takes a lot of time to do all that writing. *And,* we have to read the new entries in the notebook every week. But I suppose it's worth it. When we read the notebook, we stay up-to-date with what's going on with our clients. And sometimes there are really good sitting ideas in there, like new games to play on rainy afternoons and stuff like that.

While Jessi was writing up her job, the phone rang. We all dived for it, but I was the one to grab it first. "Hello?" I said. It was Mrs Rodowsky, phoning to see if one of us could sit for her three sons the next afternoon. I told her I'd phone her back.

Mary Anne checked the record book to see who was available. She's our club secretary, and she does a terrific job of keeping track of our schedules—Claud's art classes, my doctors' appointments, Jessi's dance lessons, and all. If she tells you that, for example, Kristy is the only one free on a Thursday afternoon, you can be sure she's right. Mary Anne has never once made a mistake. Within two minutes I was able to phone Mrs Rodowsky back and tell her that Mal would be her sitter.

You may be wondering what jobs Dawn, Jessi, and Mal have. Well, Dawn is what we call the alternate officer. That means that she is prepared to take over for any of us if we can't make a meeting. She did my job as treasurer the whole time I was back in New York, and she was good at it, too. But I don't think she enjoyed it the way I do, so Dawn was happy to give the position to me when I returned.

Jessi and Mal are what we call junior officers, which means that they can't sit at night for anybody except their own brothers and sisters. It's great to have them working in the afternoons, since that frees the rest of us to sit in the evenings.

What do we do if none of us can take a job? Well, that's where our associate members come in. We have two of them, Shannon Kilbourne and Logan Bruno. They don't come to meetings, but when we need them we can call on them. Shannon lives in Kristy's new neighbourhood, and she goes to a private school, so none of us knows her that well. She seems nice, though. And Logan—well, guess what? Logan is Mary Anne's boyfriend! They've been having some problems lately (they even broke up for a while), but we do see them together a lot. Logan is great and a good sitter. We're lucky he's in the club.

Our meeting that day went quickly. Then,

just as we were getting ready to break up, we received one last phone call. Kristy answered it, and talked for a while. When she hung up, she told us we had a new client! Her name was Mrs Gardella (Claud was the only one who'd ever heard of her—Mrs Gardella knew Claudia's mum from the library where Mrs Kishi works) and Kristy thought she must be pretty rich. That was because the Gardellas had a full-time nanny to look after their baby! But now the nanny had to go away for a few weeks ("family troubles", said Mrs Gardella), and the Gardellas desperately needed a sitter for Tara, Mouse, and Bird on Friday night. Mrs Gardella had heard "absolutely wonderful" things about our club from her friends and neighbours.

"Mouse and Bird?" asked Dawn.

"The cat and dog," said Kristy, raising her eyebrows and shrugging.

"How old is Tara?" I asked.

"Seven months," answered Kristy.

I looked at Mary Anne, who was checking the record book, and crossed my fingers. I love sitting for babies, and I was really hoping that I'd get the job. When Mary Anne glanced up, she looked straight at me. "Looks as if you've got it," she said. "You're the only one free on Friday night."

All right! New clients—and a baby. Suddenly I couldn't wait for Friday.

5th CHAPTER

I have to admit that by Friday I was a bit nervous about my job at the Gardellas'. I always feel like that the first time I sit for a new client, because there's so much I don't know. What will their house be like? Are they nice? Will the kids be angels—or monsters? Will the parents give out the information I need, or will I have to remember to ask all the right questions?

I thought about those things as I walked to their house. In fact, I was so deep in thought that I almost missed the black wrought-iron fence and gate that Mrs Gardella had told me to watch for. "Just make sure to latch the gate behind you when you come in," she'd said. "I wouldn't want Bird to get into the street."

Now that I saw the house, I remembered walking past it before. But I never thought I'd be going into it. It was a pretty impressive house: brick, with big white columns on either side of the humongous front door. A white urn stood to the right of the door, spilling over with ivy and red flowers. I opened the gate, and then carefully closed it behind me. I didn't see any dogs in the garden, but I thought it was better not to take any chances. Then I walked up the brick path and stood on the porch, looking for the doorbell.

I couldn't find it. Was I going to have to stand out there until somebody happened to open the door?

Finally, I saw this thing in the middle of the door: it was brass, and shaped kind of like a music-box key. Could that be the doorbell? I reached out and gave the key a turn. Brrring! Yup, that was it.

Immediately after the bell rang, a dog started barking ferociously. I looked through the little windows on either side of the door, and saw this huge black dog— with huge yellowish teeth! Now, I'm not usually afraid of dogs, but this one looked *mean*. I stepped back from the window, but the dog kept on barking.

"All *right*, Bird," I heard a woman's voice say. "That's enough! Go and lie down."

The door opened. "Mrs Gardella?" I said. "I'm—"

Just then the dog pushed his head into the open door, squeezed past Mrs Gardella, and jumped on me.

"Oh!" I said, surprised. For a second I was scared, but then I noticed that the dog was wagging his tail and, instead of trying to bite me, he was licking my face. "Nice dog," I said.

"Bird!" exclaimed Mrs Gardella. "Down, boy!" She grabbed his collar. "I'm so sorry," she said. "He's just too friendly, that's his problem. I keep trying to train him not to do that, but my husband actually *likes* the dog to jump up on him, so I think Bird is confused."

"It's okay," I said. I reached out to Bird. Mrs Gardella was still holding his collar, so I thought it was safe to pat him. "Hi, Bird," I said, stroking his head. "Good dog."

"Now, you must be Tracy, right?" asked Mrs Gardella.

"Um, *Stacey*," I said. I hate having to correct adults. "Stacey McGill."

"I'm sorry, Stacey," she said. "I'm terrible with names. Now, let's see. I'm ready to go but Mr Gardella is still dressing, so why don't I show you round?"

I forgot to tell you what Mrs Gardella was wearing. She was pretty dressed up—definitely more dressed up than most parents I sit for. I suppose she and her husband were going to a formal party. Mrs Gardella was wearing a tight black dress made of velvet, with a low back and long sleeves. Her shoes were velvet, too, with really high heels. She had on a diamond necklace and diamond earrings, and her black hair was pulled back with a diamond clip.

I didn't mean to stare.

"Pretty fancy, right?" Mrs Gardella said, when she caught me looking. "We're going to a party at my husband's boss's house, and it's going to be dressy. So I got out all the family jewels." She smiled.

She was nice. Even though she was rich, she was just an ordinary person. Already I liked her.

"Now," she said. "Where shall we start?" She led the way through the main hall and into a huge living room stuffed with posh furniture and expensive-looking lamps. A grand piano stood in one corner, a beautiful red silk scarf on top of it.

On top of the scarf sat a cat.

I thought Mrs Gardella would be upset about the cat sitting on that beautiful polished piano, lounging around on a piece of priceless material. But no.

"Oh, here he is," she said, walking to the cat and picking him up. "You've met Bird, now meet Mouse. How's my little Mousie?" she cooed, hugging him to her chest. His fluffy coat was leaving little white hairs all over her fancy dress, but she didn't seem to care.

"Um, hi, Mouse," I said. I wasn't sure how to talk to a cat. "He's pretty," I said to Mrs Gardella.

"Isn't he?" she asked. Just then I felt something wet pushing my hand. I almost jumped out of my skin! But when I looked down, I saw that it was only Bird, poking his nose around as if to say, "Pat me!"

"Oh, Bird is jealous," said Mrs Gardella. "You'll have to be careful about that. Whenever you give one of them attention, make sure to be fair to the other one, too. Otherwise they pick up on it and get angry and hurt."

I nodded and patted Bird.

"Now, let me show you where their food is," Mrs Gardella continued, "and I'll tell you about their dinner routine. They're used to having things done a certain way, and they get upset if their routine is disrupted." She led the way to the kitchen.

I walked behind her. I was beginning to think that she was just a little bit strange. She was talking about her pets as if they were children—and I hadn't even met the *real* baby.

"Tara's taking a late nap," Mrs Gardella called over her shoulder, as if she'd read my mind. "I'll wake her before we leave, and then she'll be up for a couple of hours. She's such a good baby. I don't think you'll have any trouble with her at all."

She showed me round the kitchen, explaining what each of the pets should be given for dinner. No canned food for *these* animals! Bird was having hamburger mixed with rice, and Mouse would be dining on chicken livers.

"Be sure to take the food out of the fridge half an hour or so before you feed them," she said. "If the food is too cold it will upset their stomachs."

She showed me Bird's bowl. It sat in the corner of their fancy dining room, placed on a little oriental rug.

"And where does Mouse eat?" I asked.

"Oh, Mousie usually joins us at the table," she said, pointing.

I looked at the huge, highly polished table. Sure enough, a small silver dish sat in the centre of the table, between two posh candlesticks. "He's been eating with us ever since he was a kitten, and I just can't bear to make him stop now."

After the kitchen/dining room tour, Mrs Gardella led me back into the living room to show me how to entertain Mouse and Bird. (She didn't seem to be worried about what I would do with Tara!) "This is Bird's favourite toy," she said, holding up a plastic hamburger. "He loves the way it squeaks." She squeezed it a couple of times, and Bird came running. Then she threw it gently across the room and he raced off after it, skidding over the big rugs and almost bashing into a glass-fronted cabinet.

Mrs Gardella laughed. "Isn't he funny?" she asked. "He loves to retrieve things.

He'll do it as long as somebody will keep throwing his toy."

"That's because he's a *bird* dog. He's bred to retrieve things," said a deep voice behind me. I turned around to see a man in a dinner jacket. "Hi, I'm Mr Gardella," he said.

"I'm Stacey," I answered.

"I suppose you've had the lowdown on these two, right?" he said.

"Yup. I think we'll have a great time."

"I just have to wake Tara, darling," said Mrs Gardella. "Then we can go." I followed her upstairs and into the baby's room. Tara was alseep in her cot. I looked around the room while Mrs Gardella woke her up. It was adorable! Everything was pink and white, with a rosebud theme. Her cot, her chest of drawers, her changing table; everything matched. Even the lampshade and the wallpaper matched.

"Hi, sweetie," I heard Mrs Gardella coo to the baby. "Time to wake up and meet Stacey." She held Tara up to see me. Tara giggled and stared at me with big blue eyes. She seemed like a happy baby, and I said so to Mrs Gardella.

"Oh, she is!" she replied. "She's *such* a happy girl, and such a good girl. I know you two will have fun together." She handed the baby to me and checked her make-up in the rosebud-trimmed mirror.

"Kay!" shouted Mr Gardella from downstairs. "We're going to be late."

44

"Coming!"

Carrying Tara, I followed Mrs Gardella downstairs. She and her husband took turns kissing the baby goodbye, and then they made a big scene over the pets.

"You be a good, good boy," said Mr Gardella to Bird while Mrs Gardella gave Mouse one last hug. "Come up and say goodbye," he added, patting his chest to show Bird what he wanted. Bird jumped up, put his front paws on Mr Gardella's chest, and licked his face.

"Oh, Peter," said Mrs Gardella. "Now you've got paw prints on your white shirt."

"Well, we match. You've got cat hair all over your dress," he answered. They laughed as they headed out the door.

I shook my head. Then I looked down at Tara. "Are you hungry?" I asked. Bird's ears perked up at the word "hungry", and Mouse started to rub against my ankles. "Okay, I suppose we're all hungry," I said. "Let's get some dinner."

It took me a while to get used to eating at such a big posh table, especially this particular big posh table, with a cat sitting in the middle of it, calmly eating chicken livers out of a silver bowl. But the dinner went smoothly, and so did the rest of the evening.

I put Tara to bed after we'd played for a while in the living room, and then I played with Mouse and Bird. Bird mainly wanted to be scratched behind the ears, and Mouse seemed to enjoy batting his toys under the sofa and then waiting for me to "rescue" them.

By the time the Gardellas came home, I was pretty tired. I felt as if I'd been sitting for three kids!

"Did Mouse eat all his dinner?" Mrs Gardella asked, just seconds after they'd walked through the door.

"Was Bird a good boy?" asked Mr Gardella.

I answered their questions while they said hello to Mouse and Bird, who seemed overjoyed to see them. Then Mrs Gardella finally asked about the baby. "Did Tara get back to sleep all right?" she said.

"She was fine," I answered. "She's a wonderful baby." Then Mr Gardella paid me (and gave me a pretty good tip) and drove me home. I had enjoyed the evening. But I couldn't help thinking that the Gardellas were a little bit weird. Really, really nice—but definitely weird.

6th CHAPTER

"Stacey." I heard someone calling my name. I tried to answer, but it was as if I were underwater; no sound came out. "Stacey, wake up!" the voice said again.

It was my mother. I struggled to wake up. My bed was so cosy, and I was snuggled down into it so comfortably. I opened one eye and looked at the clock next to my bed. Eight o'clock. Oh, no! I was going to be late for school.

Then I remembered it was Saturday. I relaxed. There was no rush. I let my eyes close again. "Stacey! Didn't you hear me call?" My mother was now standing at my bedroom door, looking impatient.

"What is it?" I asked. I love sleeping at weekends, and my mum knows that. Because she's always worrying about my health (ever since I got diabetes, that is), she lets me sleep pretty much as late as I want.

In fact, she always says that she hates to wake me when I can sleep in. So why was she waking me?

"There's a phone call for you," she said.

"Please tell whoever it is that I'll call them back," I answered. "I'm not ready to get up." I thought it must be Claud, wanting to know what my plans were for the day.

"Stacey," said my mother, "it's Mrs Gardella. And she wants to speak to you right away."

I sat up in bed. All of a sudden I was wide awake. "Mrs Gardella?" I asked.

"Yes," answered my mum. "And she sounds upset."

I got up and scrambled into my dressing gown and slippers. I was still tying the belt to my robe as I headed for the phone. Mrs Gardella! Ordinarily I'd be really annoyed if somebody phoned me so early on Saturday and interrupted my delicious extra sleep. But this call had me worried, not angry. Had I done something wrong with Tara last night? Was she ill? Or was Mouse or Bird? Or had one of them done something terrible that I should have noticed?

My heart was pounding as I grabbed the phone. "Hello?" I said.

"Stacey, this is Mrs Gardella."

"Hi," I said. "Is Tara okay?"

"She's fine—"

48

"What about Mouse? And Bird?" I asked, interrupting her.

"They're fine, too," she said. Then she paused. "But—but my jewellery isn't."

Her jewellery? I didn't know what she was talking about. Did she mean all those diamonds she was wearing the night before? I didn't say anything, because I didn't know what to say.

"Well," she continued, "I don't mean *all* my jewellery. Just the one ring. My diamond. It's missing, and I'm very upset about it."

"Diamond ring?" I repeated, sounding (I realized later) pretty stupid.

"Yes," she said. "It's a gold band, studded with little diamonds. I put it out on my dressing table last night because I was going to wear it."

"Uh-huh," I said.

"And I suppose I forgot to put it on, because you rang the bell just as I had finished dressing," she went on. "Then this morning I discovered that it had gone."

"It's gone?" I still wasn't sounding too bright. "Maybe it rolled off the dressing table?"

"We've looked everywhere. Peter—I mean, Mr Gardella—has practically turned the house upside down. We just can't find it anywhere."

Suddenly, a light switched on in my head. Was she going to accuse me—

"I hate to even suggest this, Stacey," she said, sounding embarrassed. "But could you possibly have 'borrowed' my ring? Maybe you—maybe you just wanted to show it to your friends . . ." She obviously felt almost as awkward as I did about the phone call.

"Of course I didn't borrow it!" I said loudly, without thinking. "I mean," I continued, trying to control my voice, "I didn't take your ring, Mrs Gardella. I didn't even set foot in your bedroom. The only upstairs room I was in was Tara's. I'm sorry your ring is missing, but I promise you that *I* did not take it."

Mrs Gardella cleared her throat. "Stacey," she said, "can I please speak to your mother?"

I held the phone away from my ear and looked at it. Wow. She didn't believe me. This was too much. "Mum!" I called.

"What is it?" she said, from right behind me. She must have been standing there listening the whole time. She looked worried.

I didn't feel like explaining any of it. "Mrs Gardella wants to talk to you," I said, handing her the phone.

She frowned. "Yes?" she said into the receiver.

Then she didn't say anything for a while. Mrs Gardella must have been explaining the situation to her. Mum just kept nodding. Then, finally, she started talking.

"Mrs Gardella," she began, "you don't know my daughter very well, or you would know that she's not the kind of girl who would steal anything from one of her clients' houses. Or from anyone's house!"

Then she was quiet again for a moment.

"Well," she said, after the pause, "I can't imagine where the ring is, either, but Stacey isn't a thief—or a liar. I'm sorry you feel that way."

I watched my mother's face closely while she talked. Of course, she must be remembering what I was remembering: the row we'd had the other day about a diamond ring. She was defending my honour to Mrs Gardella, but I couldn't help wondering. Was she a little bit suspicious? Did she think that, just maybe, I *could* have stolen that ring?

I felt awful.

Then my mum handed the phone back to me. Her lips were tight. "She wants to speak to you again," she said.

I took the phone. "Hello?"

"Stacey," said Mrs Gardella, "I don't know how to tell you this. I know you've denied taking the ring, and I understand why your mother feels that she has to defend you."

Of course I denied it. I didn't *do* it.

"But," she went on, "the fact remains that the ring is missing. I can't ignore that."

"Well, I'll understand if you don't want me to sit for you any more," I said quietly. "But I didn't—"

She cut me off. "It's not just you," she said. "I don't believe I'll be hiring any of the girls from your club any more."

Oh no!

"And," she continued, "I'm afraid I'm going to have to phone your other clients and let them know about this situation. It's only fair that they be warned."

I couldn't believe my ears. "Oh, please don't do that!" I said. "Our club has such a good reputation. Nothing like this has ever happened before."

"But it has happened now," said Mrs Gardella, "and, as I said, I can't ignore it."

I couldn't think of anything else to say.

"I'm sure you're a very nice girl, Stacey," she said. "But that was an expensive ring, and I have to take its loss seriously."

The phone call was over. I hung up, feeling as if I'd been punched in the stomach. Then I burst into tears.

My mother gave me a big hug. "I don't know what to say," she said. "That woman has got her mind made up, hasn't she?"

"Thanks for trying to defend me," I said through my tears.

Mum put her finger under my chin and tilted my face towards hers. "I defended you because I know you would never do such a thing," she said seriously. "I know my daughter. It's just too bad Mrs Gardella doesn't."

I told my mum what Mrs Gardella had said. "Do you really think she'll tell our other clients?" I asked.

"I hope she waits for a few days," answered Mum. "Maybe if she gives herself a chance to cool down, she'll realize she's made a mistake."

I nodded, sniffing. "I'd better phone Kristy," I said, picking up the phone. I dialled slowly, trying to control myself. Kristy wasn't going to like this one bit.

Sure enough, when I told her about my conversation with Mrs Gardella, Kristy was furious.

"How *dare* she?" she asked. "I can't believe this."

"I didn't take the ring, Kristy," I said in a small voice.

"Stacey," she answered. "I know and you know that you didn't take the ring. Don't worry about that. But what we *do* have to worry about is keeping the clients that we already have."

"How are we going to do that?" I asked.

"I don't know yet. But I do know that this calls for an emergency meeting of the BSC. Can you make it to Claud's house by midday?"

I told her I could.

"Good," she said. "I'll phone everybody else. There must be something we can do."

After we'd hung up, I went to the bathroom to wash my face. I looked at myself in the mirror. This was serious business, and I knew it. "Stacey McGill," I said to myself, "just remember this: you are *not* a thief." I nodded firmly. But I felt very, very scared.

7th CHAPTER

I was late arriving at Claud's. My morning had not gone well after the phone call from Mrs Gardella. First, when I stepped into the shower, I discovered that I was out of my favourite shampoo. Then I couldn't find any clean clothes to wear. And when I was making breakfast, I dropped an egg on the floor.

Then, just to cap everything off, when I tested my blood sugar level (something I have to do several times a day), it was high. I adjusted the amount of insulin for my injection, but I would have to keep an eye on myself for a while. Sometimes a high reading doesn't mean much at all, but sometimes it can be a warning sign.

So you can understand why I was feeling a little shaky by the time I got to the meeting.

When I walked in, everybody else was

already there. I had heard them talking while I walked up the stairs, but as soon as I opened the door, they were quiet. Had they been talking about me?

"Hi, Stacey!" chorused Jessi and Mal. They were sitting on the floor, looking rather nervous.

"Hi, Stacey," said Dawn. She was perched on the bed between Claudia and Mary Anne. The three of them seemed awfully serious.

I said hi, sat down in Claud's desk chair, and turned to look at Kristy, who hadn't said a word yet. She was in the director's chair, as usual. But she *wasn't* wearing her usual "meeting smile". In fact, she looked very, very grim.

I felt pretty grim myself.

I knew that since I hadn't taken the ring, none of this was really my fault. But I *felt* responsible for everything: for the fact that we'd had to give up our Saturday afternoon for this meeting, and for the trouble that the club was heading for.

"I'm sorry, everyone," I said quietly.

Dawn gave me a puzzled look.

"Oh, Stacey," said Kristy. "You've got nothing to be sorry for. It's not *your* fault Mrs Gardella is mad."

"She's not mad," I replied. "And I know it's not my fault. But still, I feel responsible."

"Why don't you tell us what's going on?"

Claud said impatiently to Kristy. She probably had some art project planned for the day, and now she was stuck at this meeting.

"You mean you haven't told them yet?" I asked Kristy.

"Nope, I thought you should explain, from the beginning."

Oh, my lord.

I took a deep breath and started to talk. I told my friends the whole story. I told them about the way the Gardellas treated their pets, and about how dressed up they'd been, and about Tara's fancy room. I told them that the job had gone well, and that Mr Gardella had paid me even more than I expected.

So far, so good. Everybody was interested, and I could see that nobody could guess what was coming next.

"So then," I went on, plunging ahead, "I get this phone call at the crack of dawn this morning. It was Mrs Gardella!"

"What did she want?" asked Claud.

"She wanted to know why I'd stolen her diamond ring!" I blurted it out. I felt the tears starting again, but I held them back.

"*WHAT*?" asked everybody at once.

"But I *didn't* steal it," I said quickly. I felt myself going red. I was thinking again about that birthstone ring, and I realized everybody else was, too. "I don't know *what*

57

happened to it, but I had nothing to do with the fact that it disappeared."

Suddenly everybody was talking at once, asking me questions, making comments about Mrs Gardella, and speculating on what had happened to the ring. I heard Mallory say something about what a co-incidence it was that it was the same kind of ring as the one I'd seen at the arcade. But it was just a casual comment. I knew she didn't mean anything by it.

"Hold on, hold on," yelled Kristy over the noise. "Let's let Stacey finish her story."

So I told them about the phone call. I told them exactly what Mrs Gardella had said about the missing ring, and exactly what I'd said. And what my mother had said. It didn't take long.

Finally I got to the worst part, the part that was hardest to tell.

"And then, she said that not only did she not want *me* to sit for her again, but that she wouldn't hire *anybody* from the club."

"So what?" said Claud. "Who wants to sit for them, anyway?" Claudia's a great best friend. She's always so loyal. I gave her a grateful look.

But then I had to tell them the rest. "And she said she was going to phone our other clients and tell them what had happened."

There was silence in the room. Everybody looked totally stunned.

"How awful," whispered Dawn. "Nothing like this has ever happened before. What about the club's reputation?"

Mary Anne elbowed her in the side. "Dawn!" she said. "Can't you see that Stacey feels bad enough already?" Good old Mary Anne. You can count on her to be sensitive about other people's feelings. But Dawn was right.

"Dawn's right," I said out loud. "It *is* awful. But I don't know what we can do about it."

"What if we phone all our clients first, and explain what really happened?" asked Jessi, thoughtfully.

"That might just stir up more trouble," answered Kristy. "I mean, what if Mrs Gardella *doesn't* end up phoning everybody? Then we would have brought up the problem for nothing and confused our clients."

"Yeah," agreed Claud. "If you go out of your way to insist that you're innocent, people are going to wonder if you're actually guilty." Claud knows about that sort of stuff because of all those Nancy Drew books she reads.

"What if we try to convince Mrs Gardella not to make the calls?" asked Dawn. She looked at me hopefully.

"I don't think we can talk her out of it if her mind's made up," I answered. I felt miserable. "I mean, she thinks it's the right

59

thing to do, and in a way, she's right. If I *had* stolen something, people should know about it."

"But you didn't," said Kristy. "Don't even talk like that. It's *not* the right thing for her to do—it's like she's assuming that you're guilty. You're supposed to be innocent until proven guilty, right?"

"Right," I answered. "Let's hope our other clients go along with that kind of thinking."

"You know," said Mary Anne, "I bet they will. After all, most of our clients have been hiring us for a long time. They know we're honest. They know we would never steal."

"I hope you're right, Mary Anne," said Kristy. "Because our good reputation is the only thing we've got going for us right now. There's not much we can do about Mrs Gardella."

I spent the rest of Saturday and all day Sunday hoping the whole thing would blow over without affecting the club. On Monday, school dragged. I was eager to get to our meeting that afternoon.

Finally, it was 5:30. Kristy called the meeting to order, and then I collected the subs. We talked for a while about what we had done over the weekend. We talked about what had happened at school that day (nothing much, in case you're wondering).

We even talked about the weather (clear and crisp—we agreed that it had been a very nice day). We talked about everything except Mrs Gardella and the missing diamond ring. And the whole time we were talking, what we were *really* doing was waiting for the phone to ring.

But it didn't.

I stared at the silent phone, wondering if there could be any other explanation. But I couldn't come up with anything. I checked the clock. Five-forty. Usually by that time we would have got at least one or two calls.

Our conversation lagged. Nobody had anything left to say, it seemed. Then, suddenly, the phone rang. We all dived for it, but I got it. "Hello?" I said eagerly. "Babysitters Club."

"Oh, sorry," said a voice on the other end. "I was trying to reach the sewage treatment plant. Wrong number, I suppose."

Any other time, I would have told everyone else what the woman had said, and we would have giggled over it for the rest of the meeting. But that day I didn't feel very funny, so I just said, "Wrong number," and put the phone down.

"Hmmm," said Kristy.

"What do you mean by *that*?" I asked. I felt she was trying to tell me something. "Maybe you think I should leave the club. Is that what you think?"

"Stacey, are you nuts?" she exclaimed. "I don't want you to leave the club. And I don't blame you for anything. All I said was, 'Hmmm'."

I suppose I was feeling a little jumpy.

We sat quietly for a few more minutes. I could hear Claud's digital clock clicking the minutes away. Soon the meeting would be over. Finally, at 5:48 (I know the exact time, since I was watching the clock so closely), the phone rang again. This time I let somebody else answer it.

"Hello?" said Kristy. "Oh, hi, Mrs Braddock." She listened for a moment. "I'm sure we can fit you in," she said, giving the rest of us a little smile. "I'll call you back in a couple of minutes." When she'd hung up, she told us that Mrs Braddock needed a sitter for Haley and Matt.

"Did she sound—weird at all?" I asked. "Like she might have heard any rumours or anything?" We've been sitting for the Braddocks for a long time. I wondered what Mrs Braddock would think if Mrs Gardella phoned her.

"She didn't, really," said Kristy. "And I didn't want to ask. I wonder if she's heard anything. Maybe she has, but she doesn't believe it."

"Well, anyway," said Mary Anne, looking at the record book. "We can certainly fit her in. We do have a few jobs that we lined up last week, but basically we're wide open.

62

You're available, Kristy, and so are Stacey, Jessi, and Dawn."

"I don't want the job," I said quickly. Somehow I didn't feel that I should take any jobs when there were so few of them. The others worked it out among themselves, and Kristy called Mrs Braddock back.

After that, we only got one other phone call, from Mrs Newton. She's another of our long-time clients. She didn't sound any different than usual either. At least, not according to Claud, who had answered the phone. Once that job was set up, it was six o'clock and time for the meeting to end.

Was it just coincidence that we'd had such a slow meeting? There was no way of knowing. We'd have to wait and see what happened next. I decided to keep my fingers crossed for at least the next few days.

8th CHAPTER

Tuesday

Oh, boy. WARNING! There's a new kid on the block. On Burnt Hill Road, that is. And this little terror might just be a challenger to the "walking disaster" title that Jackie Rodowsky now holds. His name's Joey Conklin, and all I can say is <u>watch out</u>. He's a cute kid, and I don't think he means to cause chaos, but.... Anyway, I wasn't even sitting for him! I was sitting for Jenny and Andrea, and everything was going fine, until Mr. Trouble showed up.

Mary Anne is usually pretty sensible when it comes to dealing with difficult kids, so when I started to read her notebook entry, I knew that this Joey must really be something.

But, as she said, her day started off well. She was sitting for the Prezziosos that afternoon. Jenny Prezzioso is four, and she can be kind of a b-r-a-t. She's used to getting her own way, and she can be very definite about what "her way" means. I think she's starting to grow out of her spoiled phase a little, though. Ever since Andrea arrived, Jenny's had to be the big sister.

We were all worried about how well Jenny would cope with having a new baby sister. We thought we were in for the biggest case of sibling rivalry in the history of the world. But Jenny surprised us. She *adores* Andrea, loves to help looking after her, and is one of the sweetest, most gentle big sisters I've ever seen.

"Hello, Mary Anne," said Mrs Prezzioso, answering the door. "I'm so glad you're a few minutes early. My meeting time got changed, and I've really got to rush if I'm going to make it."

"No problem," said Mary Anne. She's almost always early—all of us are. You never know when parents are going to need a little extra time to tell you something about the kids, or finish dressing, or give

65

you instructions about where to get hold of them in an emergency.

Mrs Prezzioso was getting her jacket out of the hall cupboard. "Andrea's napping, but she should be up in a half hour or so. And Jenny's—"

"Hi, Mary Anne!" said Jenny, bounding into the room.

"There's Jenny now," said Mrs Prezzioso. "Goodbye, darling." She kissed Jenny. "Be good for Mary Anne. I'll be back soon." She grabbed her car keys and ran out of the door.

Jenny looked excited. She hardly seemed to notice that her mother had left. "Guess what! It's almost my birthday," she said with a big smile.

"It is?" asked Mary Anne. As far as she remembered, Jenny's birthday was months away. But kids always seem to think that their birthdays are just around the corner.

"Yup!" said Jenny. "And guess how old I'm going to be?"

"Ummm . . . forty-five?" asked Mary Anne.

"No, silly!" shrieked Jenny, giggling. "I'm going to be thirteen."

"Now *you're* being silly," said Mary Anne. "*I'm* thirteen. You're four."

"I know I'm four now," said Jenny. "But on my birthday I'm going to be thirteen."

"Sorry, Jenny," said Mary Anne. "I

think you might have to try being five, first."

Jenny frowned.

"Anyway," said Mary Anne, "I think your birthday is still pretty far away." She noticed that Jenny was frowning even harder, and decided to avoid a scene. "But how about if we have a pretend birthday party today?" she continued, quickly. "We'll dress up, and invite all your dolls— and Andrea, too, of course—and have pretend cake and pretend presents. Okay?"

Jenny was jumping up and down with excitement. "A birthday party! A birthday party!" she yelled.

"Shhh," Mary Anne said. "Let's try not to wake Andrea until the party's all ready. Now, let's find a couple of presents to wrap up." Jenny cruised around the living room and chose three of her favourite toys: a Barbie (the one she calls "Hospital Barbie" because she got it when Mrs P was in hospital having Andrea), a ratty old clown doll she calls Mr Bog, and her find-the-picture book.

While she was looking, Mary Anne had found last Saturday's comics and a roll of tape. "Ready to wrap them?" she asked. They sat on the living room floor and Mary Anne helped Jenny wrap her "gifts". Jenny became intent on her job. She wrinkled her brow and stuck her tongue out of the corner of her mouth. It was pretty cute, according to Mary Anne. Finally Jenny had finished. *Covered* with a million pieces of tape, but finished.

Meanwhile, Mary Anne had cut a cake out of a piece of cardboard. "Want to draw the decorations and the candles?" she asked Jenny. Jenny jumped up to find her crayons.

"Okay," said Mary Anne. "It looks like we're ready for our party. What do you want to wear?" They trooped up to Jenny's room to look over the possibilities. Jenny has quite a wardrobe. Her mother has always liked to dress her up like a "little princess". She has tons of dresses, all dripping with lace and floppy bows and satin ribbons. She's got party shoes in every colour and style you can imagine. And she has posh tights with ruffles on the seat and polka-dot decorations.

In other words, it's no problem finding something for Jenny to dress up in.

But Mary Anne had to stifle a giggle when she saw what Jenny had chosen to wear to her party. She'd rummaged around in her chest of drawers until she found a faded pair of dungarees and a pink-striped sweatshirt that was a little too small. Then she chose a pair of pink trainers.

"Are you sure that's what you want to wear?" she asked Jenny, and Jenny nodded firmly. "Okay, then," said Mary Anne.

"Time to wake up Andrea and get the other guests to the party."

Jenny stayed in her room, rounding up her favourite dolls and stuffed animals. Mary Anne went to Andrea's room and found her already awake. She wasn't crying, or even looking unhappy. She was just relaxing in her cot, looking around the room with a big smile on her face.

"You look as if you're ready for a party," said Mary Anne, picking her up. "As soon as I put a dry nappy on you, that is," she added, wrinkling her nose. Mary Anne laid Andrea on the changing table, and immediately Andrea broke into a loud wail. Jenny came running.

"Don't cry, Andrea!" she exclaimed. "We're going to have a birthday party, and you're invited." Andrea continued to cry. "Wait a minute," said Jenny. She ran out of the room. Two seconds later, she popped back in. This time she was holding a stuffed monkey. "Here, Andrea. Here's Monkey Matthew," she said. "Now do you feel better?"

Andrea's wails grew louder. Mary Anne struggled with the nappy's plastic tapes, trying to unfasten them. As Mary Anne worked at changing Andrea, Jenny kept running back and forth, bringing toys that she thought would cheer up her sister. It was a nice thing for a big sister to do, said

Mary Anne later, but unfortunately, none of the toys did the trick.

Andrea finally stopped crying when Mary Anne finished with her nappy. Then Jenny helped choose an outfit for her to wear to the party. Andrea's outfit was a little fancier than Jenny's. Jenny chose a pink nightdress with lace trim, and a "princess" crown from the dressing-up box.

"She looks so beautiful," said Jenny. "Maybe it should be *Andrea's* birthday that we're having the party for."

"Great idea," said Mary Anne. They headed downstairs and into the kitchen. Mary Anne poured some orange juice for Jenny to have with her pretend cake. Andrea got a bottle. Jenny sang "Happy Birthday" five times for her sister, becoming louder and more off-key with each version.

Then Jenny "helped" Andrea open her presents. Even though she'd wrapped them only minutes ago, Jenny shrieked with surprise as each present was opened.

"These presents are only pretend, though," she reminded Andrea seriously. "You can play with them for today, but they're really still *my* toys."

Andrea smiled and said, "Glug."

"You're welcome," said Jenny. "Now can we play outside?" she asked, turning to Mary Anne.

Mary Anne nodded. "As soon as we clear

up from our party," she said, picking up the "wrapping paper" and putting the "cake" aside.

It was a beautiful day outside, and Mary Anne relaxed on the porch with Andrea while Jenny performed "ballet" on the front lawn. Then Mary Anne saw a little boy peeping through the bushes at the edge of the lawn. He was watching Jenny, and it was obvious that he wanted to play. He seemed a little shy, though. "Hi!" Mary Anne called. "What's your name?"

"That's Joey, silly!" yelled Jenny. "Hi, Joey! Want to play tag?"

Soon Jenny and Joey were running happily around the garden, shrieking with laughter as they fought over who was "It". Andrea sat happily in Mary Anne's lap, watching them play.

Then she got restless. She squirmed and wriggled and kicked. "Okay, Andrea,' said Mary Anne. "I get the message. You're bored." She stood up, holding Andrea, and walked around the garden, singing softly to her.

She walked up and down the side garden until Andrea's eyes began to close. "Ready for another nap?" she said. "Okay, let's go inside." Mary Anne looked for Jenny and Joey, planning to invite them inside, too, but they were nowhere to be seen. Mary Anne's heart began to pound. How could she have lost two kids? She'd been

71

looking right at them just a couple of minutes ago.

"Jenny!" she called. "Joey!" She walked round to the front door—until she saw something that made her hurry. It was a hose, the garden hose that was usually coiled up behind some shrubbery next to the porch. Only now, it ran from the outside tap, over the lawn, through the shrubs, onto the porch, and through the front door!

That hose couldn't be on, Mary Anne said to herself as she ran, holding Andrea carefully. It just couldn't. She threw open the front door and stopped short. There was Jenny, laughing wildly. There was Joey, holding the hose. And there was water—all over *everything*. Joey was watering the front hall and its furniture.

Mary Anne was stunned. For a moment she didn't even know what to say. Then she did. "Joey!" she said loudly. "Get that hose out of the house. Now!" She rushed over to him and guided him out of the door. "Now turn off the tap," she added, watching him from the porch. Joey ran to the tap.

"And now," she said, "I think it's time for you to go home." Joey looked at her with big eyes. So far, he hadn't said a word. He turned to leave the garden. "Wait a minute, Joey," called Mary Anne. "What's your last name? I want to phone your mummy."

"Ummm," said Joey. He looked around, pretending not to know it.

72

"Conklin!" said Jenny from behind Mary Anne. "His last name is Conklin."

"Thank you, Jenny," Mary Anne replied. "Goodbye, Joey Conklin." She walked back into the front hall, still carrying Andrea. "Oh, boy," she said, looking at all the water. "Oh, boy."

She spent most of the rest of the day undoing what Joey had done. First, she put Andrea down for a nap, since Andrea had been getting sleepy anyway. Then she phoned Mrs Conklin. Then she settled Jenny with some crayons and paper. Then she got out the mop. It was a long afternoon.

9th
CHAPTER

"No, I don't think there was any permanent damage," said Mary Anne. "Except maybe to my nerves. Can you imagine? Watch out for that Joey."

The members of the BSC had been talking about Mary Anne's experience at the Prezziosos'. It was 5:35 on Wednesday, and Kristy had called our meeting to order. Nobody had brought up the situation with the Gardellas, and I was glad. I'd been thinking about it for days, and I needed a break.

Claudia, Dawn, and Mary Anne were sprawled on Claud's bed, munching popcorn labelled "Clever food". Kristy was perched in the director's chair, as usual. I was sitting on the floor that day, with my back against the bed, facing Jessi and Mal. They were looking through a book of Claud's called *The Horse in Art*.

"Why do you think they call it Clever food, anyway?" asked Claud. "I mean, how can popcorn make you clever?" She threw a handful into her mouth. "Even if it is incredibly delicious."

"I don't think they mean it makes you clever," said Mary Anne. "I think they mean that you're clever if you buy it. Because it's a healthy snack—I mean, compared to Hula Hoops or something."

"Let me try some," said Mal. "If there's any chance that it does make you clever, I should eat loads of it. I have a maths test tomorrow and I don't think I'm going to understand any of the *questions*, much less come up with the right answers."

At that moment I realized something was wrong. Ordinarily, Kristy would not put up with "non-club" conversation going on for so long. She makes us concentrate on club business between 5:30 and 6:00. But that day she didn't seem to be paying attention to the chatter that was going on. She was just staring at the phone with this fierce expression on her face, as if she could make it ring.

But it sat there silently.

I started to worry. I didn't think I could stand it if I had to sit through another meeting where nobody (or hardly anybody) phoned us. I began to stare at the phone, too. And after a little more conversation about the good points and bad points of various kinds of junk food (Claud's favourite subject), everybody else shut up, too. So there we were, all seven of us, sitting in Claud's room and staring at a quiet phone.

Then it rang.

"All right!" yelled Kristy. She composed herself quickly and picked up the phone. "Babysitters Club," she said. We watched her carefully as she spoke to the person on the other end. It's always fun to try to guess who the caller is, just by listening to one end of the conversation.

"Of course, Mrs Sobak," Kristy said after a while. "I understand. Wednesday at 4:30. That's fine."

Well, we didn't have to guess any more. Mrs Sobak must have been phoning for a sitter for Betsy, her eight-year-old daughter. As Kristy hung up, Mary Anne pulled out the record book, a puzzled expression on her face. "Haven't we already—" she began to ask.

"Yup," said Kristy. "We have already arranged that job. I was supposed to take it. But Mrs Sobak wasn't calling to hire us. She was calling to cancel."

Everybody gasped. "Cancel?" asked Dawn. "Why?"

I squeezed my eyes shut, wishing that I could cover my ears, too. I didn't want to hear what I thought Kristy was going to say, that Mrs Sobak had talked to Mrs Gardella and didn't want to use our club any more.

"Betsy's uncle is coming to town," said Kristy. "And Mrs Sobak wants Betsy to have a chance to see him. He's going to take her to the zoo that afternoon."

I let out a breath. "Really?" I asked. What a relief.

"Well, that's what she said," answered Kristy. She sounded a bit doubtful. "Who knows if that's the *real* reason?"

My stomach flip-flopped. I felt *so* guilty, even though this wasn't really my fault.

"Do you think the real reason could be that Mrs Gar—" began Mal, but Jessi elbowed her in the ribs.

"Shh," she said. "Don't even say it."

Everybody was quiet again after that. And the phone was quiet, too. I was beginning to feel sick. Our meetings are usually so much fun, but this one was a disaster.

"This is the worst," said Dawn suddenly. "What are we going to do?"

"I don't know," said Kristy. "But you know what? I was thinking last night that this club has been through some pretty bad times before, and we've always managed to come out on top. I'm sure we'll work out this problem, too."

She sounded pretty certain. I wasn't so confident.

"What's the worst thing that's ever happened to the club?" asked Jessi. She looked interested. "I mean, if you don't mind talking about it."

We thought for a minute.

"It was when—" began Mary Anne.

"It must have been—" said Dawn at the same time.

"You go ahead," said Mary Anne.

"No, you," said Dawn. "You've been in the club longer."

"Well," said Mary Anne. "I was going to say that the worst time *I* remember was when we had that humongous fight and none of us was speaking to the others. Remember?"

Kristy, Claudia, and I all nodded. "Boy, do I remember. Believe it or not," I said to Jessi, "we were all so angry with each other that we couldn't even stand to be in the same room. So instead of having meetings—"

"We each took turns sitting here alone answering the phone!" finished Kristy. "Oh, that was so ridiculous."

"What was the row *about*?" asked Mallory. "I was thinking about it last night, and I couldn't even remember."

"I remember," said Dawn quietly. "I hadn't joined the club yet, but that row happened right before I joined. In fact, Mary Anne and I met because she had nobody to sit with at lunch! I was new in town, so we were both feeling lonely. Of course, I didn't know at first that she *did* actually have friends, but that she wasn't speaking to any of them at the time."

"So what was the fight about?" asked Jessi.

"Well," said Dawn, "it was to do with the way we sometimes used to take jobs without checking first to see who was available."

"Job-hogging!" yelled Claudia. "Now I remember. And Mary Anne told us all off. Can you believe it?"

"That's right," said Kristy. "Job-hogging. But then we kept getting angrier and angrier at each other for all kinds of other reasons, and by the time we were finally ready to make up, we couldn't even be sure who needed to apologize to whom for what."

"So we had a group apology," I said. "Want to show them what we did?" I asked the others. "Ready? One, two, three—"

"I'm sorry!" Claud, Kristy, Mary Anne, and I chorused at once. Then we cracked up. We were laughing so hard that we almost didn't hear the phone ring. Jessi grabbed it.

"Hello?" she said. "Oh, hello, Mrs Addison, how are you?" She paused for a moment. "I'm sorry to hear that," she went on, looking glum. "I hope you both feel better soon. Thanks for calling." She hung up and looked around the room.

"You're not going to believe this," she said. "Mrs Addison has just cancelled, too."

"You're kidding!" said Claud. "That was *my* job. On Saturday night, right?"

"Right," answered Jessi. "She and her husband were supposed to go to the theatre. But now she and Corrie have got sore throats, and the doctor said she should avoid being in public, since they could have flu and be contagious."

"Oh, no!" said Claud. "I really needed that job, too. I'm broke." She looked depressed.

"Hey Kristy, tell us about another rough time," said Mallory. I think she was trying to change the subject and get our minds off what was happening.

"Well," began Kristy, thinking.

"I know," I said. "What about the time those girls started the Babysitters Agency and tried to steal our clients?"

"Oh, my lord," said Claud. "That really was the worst. Remember, Kristy? You wanted us to try to compete with them by lowering our prices and offering house-cleaning services for no extra charge."

"*What*?" said Jessi and Mal at the same time.

"Don't worry," said Kristy. "They talked me out of it. And the Agency self-destructed because the sitters they hired were so terrible."

"But you know what?" said Claud. "I've just remembered. They *did* steal some of our clients—for a while. And during that time, we'd have meetings when the phone never rang. Just like now."

"You're right," said Mary Anne. "And we survived that, didn't we?" She sounded optimistic. But then she looked down at the record book. "I have to say, though, that things don't look too good. We hardly have any jobs arranged for the next week. And the ones we *do* have are mostly for the Pikes and the Ramseys and the Brewers."

Were we reduced to sitting only for our families? This didn't look good. But we spent the last few minutes of the meeting talking about other bad times the club had been through, and by the end of it I felt a bit better. The phone hadn't rung again, but at least I had the feeling that things might work out. I had no idea *how*, but I was hoping for the best.

10th CHAPTER

Thursday

I never thought that sitting for my own brother and sister could be so exciting. Exciting? Well, maybe terrifying is the word I'm looking for. Luckily, Becca and Squirt never had any idea how truly frightened I was. And I'm kind of proud of myself for managing to hide my fear.

Jessi was sitting for Becca and Squirt on Thursday night. Her parents had gone to a dinner party, and her Aunt Cecelia, who lives with them, had gone to the cinema. Jessi says she always has a good time sitting for Becca and Squirt, but she doesn't get to do it very often now, since Aunt Cecelia came to live with the Ramseys. Jessi's aunt would probably prefer to be the full-time sitter for the Ramseys, since she thinks she's the only one who knows the right way to do things. But once in a while, Jessi gets lucky and Aunt Cecelia has plans on the same night Mr and Mrs Ramsey do.

"Hey, Squirt," said Jessi. "Let me see your ba." "Ba" is what Squirt calls his belly button, and he loves pulling up his shirt to show it off. You should see his grin when he does it. He looks so, so proud of himself. It's a riot.

They were sitting around in the living room after dinner (Jessi had made hot dogs and beans, Becca's favourite), listening to the radio, and trying to decide what to do next. Becca wanted to play Cluedo, but Jessi vetoed that idea.

"We have to play something we can play together," she said. "Squirt can't play Cluedo."

"Squirt can't play *anything*," said Becca. "He's just a baby."

"Well, maybe he can't play any board games, but if we think, I'm sure we can come up with some kind of game Squirt can play." Jessi and Becca sat quietly for a few minutes, thinking. Squirt continued to show off his ba, even though nobody was paying attention.

"I know," said Jessi. She picked up a button that had been lying on the table. It had fallen off her father's shirt just as her parents were getting ready to leave.

"Let's play a new kind of hide-and-seek. I'll hide this button somewhere in the room, and then you try to find it. Squirt loves to look for things, so he'll have a good time."

"What happens when I find it?" asked Becca. She didn't sound convinced that the game would be fun.

"Then you get to hide it and I'll look," answered Jessi.

"Okay," said Becca. "Let's try it. I'll close my eyes while you hide the button." She scrunched up her eyes and held Squirt on her lap. "Close your eyes, Squirt," she said. "Like me." Squirt scrunched up his eyes, too.

Jessi looked round the room. The Ramseys' living room isn't all that big, but there are plenty of places where you can hide something as little as a button. She didn't want to make the game too hard, though, because then Becca would get frustrated.

Finally, she put it underneath one of the magazines stacked on the coffee table.

"Ready!" she said, as soon as she'd made sure the magazines were back in their original positions.

Becca opened her eyes and started to roam around the room. Squirt followed her, picking up everything that she picked up, looking into every corner that she looked into, poking his fingers between the sofa cushions the same way she did. He was having a great time.

Jessi watched as Becca narrowed down the hiding places. But every time Becca approached the coffee table, she'd get distracted by another idea and look somewhere else. Jessi wanted to giggle, but she controlled herself. She knew the game wasn't easy. She waited patiently, singing along to the song that was on the radio.

Finally, Becca went to the coffee table and started to pick up each magazine in turn. "I've found it!" she squealed, when she turned over the one that was hiding the button. "I found it, Squirt."

Squirt squealed, too. He was almost as happy as Becca was.

"Okay," said Jessi. "Now, let's go to another room and *you* get to hide the button." They trooped into the kitchen. "Hey," said Jessi, when they got there, "I know. Instead of hiding a button in this room, let's hide this." She held up a little bottle opener. "We'll use a different object in each room."

"Close your eyes!" commanded Becca, and Jessi closed her eyes. She heard the fridge door open and shut, and then the sound of cupboard doors closing. She heard the rustle of paper bags. Then it was quiet. "Okay," said Becca.

Jessi and Squirt began to search the kitchen. They looked in every corner, and under every appliance. They looked in the sink, and they even checked the oven. Jessi opened the fridge and peeped inside. No bottle opener. Finally, she opened the cutlery drawer. There was the opener, where it was usually kept!

Becca giggled. "Good trick, right?" she asked.

"Good trick," agreed Jessi. "You know, I think it took me a lot longer to find that than it took you to find the button. We should time our searches so we know who's faster. That would really make the game good." She dug around in a drawer and found the egg timer. "This will work," she said. "Let's go into the dining room."

They played for quite a while. Jessi hid Squirt's favourite toy—a blue plastic fish—in the dining room, and then Becca hid a toothbrush in the bathroom. Jessi hid one of her ballet shoes in her bedroom, and then Becca hid her Barbie in *her* bedroom. Squirt trailed along everywhere they went, giggling happily whenever an object was

86

found. *He* never found anything, but he didn't seem to care.

The girls timed their searches to see who was faster, and Becca kept winning. "You're good at this game, Becca," said Jessi.

"I like looking for things," replied Becca. "This is fun."

Then they went into their parents' room. It was Jessi's turn to hide something, and she chose one of her mother's earrings from her dressing table. While Becca closed her eyes, Jessi looked for a good place. An earring was so small she could put it almost anywhere.

"Hey, wait a minute," she said out loud.

Becca opened her eyes. "What?" she asked.

"I'm just thinking . . ." said Jessi. "Never mind. Close your eyes again." She hid the earring under a pillow and then watched while Becca searched. And as she watched, she thought. While she had been looking for a place, she'd suddenly realized how many hiding places there could be in a house. And then she thought of Mrs Gardella's ring. She'd known all along that I hadn't stolen it, but now she had some ideas about what might have happened to it. It could easily have been misplaced. It could be anywhere!

As soon as Becca found the earring, Jessi hurried her sister and brother downstairs. She was planning to phone me and tell me what she'd been thinking. Maybe the

Gardellas simply hadn't looked hard enough. Becca and Squirt ran into the kitchen to find a snack. Jessi followed them. But as she walked through the living room, she was stopped in her tracks by something she heard on the radio. It was a news flash, and since she was listening to WSTO—the Voice of Stoneybrook—she knew it must be local news. The word that had made her stop and listen was "thief".

"A professional and possibly dangerous thief is still at large in the area," said the announcer. "Police report that he has broken into several homes in the past two weeks, and they've had calls reporting three burglaries tonight alone. Homeowners are warned to lock their doors and windows, hide their valuables, and take other precautions. Anyone who has information on the matter should call the police at—"

Jessi snapped off the radio. She glanced around. She could hear her brother and sister laughing in the kitchen. Phew. At least Becca hadn't heard about the thief.

But Jessi was terrified. There was a burglar on the loose in Stoneybrook, and he could be looking into the living room window at that very moment! Uh-oh, she thought. What am I going to do now?

Her first thought, she told me later, was to phone her parents. She knew they'd come straight home, and then everything would be okay. No burglar was going to rob a home that was full of people, and anyway, she'd feel safer if her parents were there. But she threw away that thought in a second. If she called her parents, she would prove to Aunt Cecelia (who would be sure to hear about it later) that Jessi wasn't "mature" enough to sit for Becca and Squirt. Then she'd *never* get to sit for them.

Jessi pulled herself together. The thing to do, she realized, would be to make the house as secure as possible—but without letting Becca and Squirt know what she was doing. She began by checking to see that all the windows were locked. She tried the living room windows, and then went into the kitchen and checked those.

"What are you doing, Jessi?" asked Becca.

"Oh, well . . ." said Jessi, thinking fast. "It just seems as if it might be getting a bit chilly outside, and I wanted to be sure the windows were closed tight."

"Can I help?" asked Becca.

"Of course," said Jessi, and she and Becca (with Squirt following along) walked through the house checking windows. Jessi also checked the doors, when Becca wasn't looking.

"We should be pretty warm now," said Becca, after they'd checked the last window.

"Right," said Jessi. "But . . . doesn't it seem a bit dark and gloomy in here? Let's turn on some more lights." She realized the burglar wouldn't want to break into a house that was all lit up, so she went from room to room, turning on every light. Her father would kill her when the electric bill came, but she thought it was worth it.

"Let's help Mama tidy up," she said, when they had reached her parents' bedroom. She swept her mother's jewellery off the top of her dressing table and into a drawer. After all, the newscaster had said to "hide valuables". What other valuables did they have?

She thought for a minute. "You know," she said to Becca, who was beginning to look at her with a puzzled expression, "since we're not watching the TV, maybe we should cover it up. It'll look neater. The VCR, too."

Jessi threw a blanket over the TV and VCR. "Now," she said. "Let's have some music." She flicked on the radio and found a station playing rock music. Then she turned up the volume as loud as it would go. She wanted to make absolutely sure the thief would know that someone was at home.

"Let's dance!" exclaimed Jessi. She grabbed Squirt, swung him up, and danced him around the living room. Becca gave her a funny look, but then her favourite song came on and she shrugged and started dancing, too.

In the middle of the song, Jessi had an

awful thought. Could the *thief* have stolen Mrs Gardella's ring? Could he have been in the house while Stacey was babysitting? "Oh, my lord," she said out loud—but nobody heard her because the music was so loud. That was the scariest thing Jessi could imagine.

When Mrs and Mr Ramsey came home, they found Jessi reading on the sofa, with the radio on—loudly. Becca and Squirt had managed to fall asleep, but every light in the house was on, including the ones in their rooms.

Jessi explained the situation to her parents, and they told her they were proud of her. Then she went to bed. Now that they were at home, she felt safe as she drifted off to sleep. And her last thought before she slept made her smile. If the thief *had* taken the ring, she thought, then Stacey's name would be cleared. And the Babysitters Club would be back to normal business.

11th CHAPTER

Saturday

I reely do apresh apprish apreciate — I'm realy greatful to you lot for leting me have the job at the Pretziosa's, sinse my other job at the Adison's got canseled. I relly do need the money these days. Even if it meens sitting for Genny, who can be sush a pane. (You were rite, though, Mary Anne — she has got better latley.) But I wuld have liked to stay their for more than just an hour and a half. I was counting on being paid for at leest three. Now I'm going to have to return those pink trainers. If I want to by any art supplies this month, that is.

Claud isn't usually so obsessed with how much money she makes. Most of us babysit because it's fun, not because it makes us millionaires. But we have begun to count on the money we make, and now that we weren't getting so many jobs, Claud was feeling the pinch.

The call from Mrs Prezzioso had come during Friday's meeting. It was one of the only calls we'd got.

"I wonder," Kristy had said after she'd hung up. "Do you think the Prezziosos just haven't heard the Gardella story?"

"Maybe they have but they're desperate for a sitter," Dawn had said. "Anyway, who gets the job?"

Mary Anne checked the record book. "Well, the only ones free are Claud, Kristy, Mal, and Stacey."

I didn't want the job, because I still felt guilty about what had happened. And Kristy and Mal had said they were still getting jobs sitting for their brothers and sisters, so they didn't need the money as much as Claud did. Claud had accepted the job gratefully.

So there she was that Saturday night, saying goodbye to Mr and Mrs Prezzioso as they headed out for a party. They were all dressed up and Mrs P was "reeking of perfume", as Claud said later. They really seemed to be looking forward to their night out.

"Okay, Jenny," said Claud, after they'd left. "Let's get your little sister ready for bed."

"Can I choose her pyjamas?" asked Jenny.

"Okay," Claud answered. She led the way to Andrea's room. "Which ones do you want her to wear?"

Jenny picked out a pair of blue pyjamas with pink dinosaurs on them. "These are her favourite ones," she said. She helped Claud put a nappy on Andrea and then put on the pyjamas. ("Helping" meant mostly just standing around and saying, "Mummy doesn't do it like that," and other useful things.)

Then they went back downstairs to get a bottle for Andrea. Mrs Prezzioso had left one in the bottle warmer, so it was all ready. They trooped back to Andrea's room. Claud sat in the rocking chair with the baby, hoping that the motion would help her to fall asleep once she'd finished her bottle.

Jenny ran into her own room and found her favourite doll, then dragged her little children's-sized rocking chair into Andrea's room and put it next to the big chair. "I'm going to put *my* baby to bed, too," she said. She tipped a doll's bottle towards her "baby's" mouth, and held the doll while she rocked slowly.

Claud started singing softly to Andrea. "Hush, little baby, don't say a word."

Jenny sang to her baby, too. "'Twinkle, twinkle, little star.'" It wasn't exactly a lullaby, but it was a song she knew.

Claudia and Jenny rocked next to each other until Claud noticed that Andrea's eyes were drooping. "Oh, you're getting sleepy, aren't you?" she said. She put down the bottle and lifted Andrea to her shoulder, patting her on the back.

Jenny burped her baby, too.

Then Claud gently lowered Andrea into her cot. "Go to sleep now," she said, rubbing Andrea's back softly.

Jenny put her doll on the floor in a little nest she'd made of blankets. "Time to sleep," she said, rubbing the doll's back.

Then Claud and Jenny tiptoed out of the room. "You're a good mummy," said Claud.

"I know," said Jenny. "I watch what *my* mummy does and I do the same things."

"What's your baby's name?" asked Claud. She was expecting maybe Ashley or Melissa.

"Pee-wee," answered Jenny seriously.

Claud had to stifle a giggle.

"He's my favourite on TV, so I named my baby after him," explained Jenny.

Claud kept a straight face and nodded. "Well, Pee-wee is a very good baby," she said. "Now, what would you like to do until bedtime?"

"Let's play house," said Jenny. "You can

be the mummy and I'll be the little baby."
She crouched on the floor and started to
crawl around.

Claudia smiled. She knows that older
brothers and sisters sometimes like to play
"baby" so they can get the same kind of
attention their siblings are getting. "Does
the baby want a bottle?" she asked.

"Waaa!" answered Jenny. "Baby want a
bottle."

Claudia went into the kitchen and put
some apple juice into an empty bottle.
"Here you go," she said, bringing it to
Jenny. Jenny crawled into Claud's lap and
started drinking out of the bottle. Then she
wriggled out again. "Waa!" she said. "Baby
wants toys."

Claud pulled a few of Andrea's baby toys
out of the toy basket. "Here you go, baby,"
she said, giving them to Jenny. Jenny took
them and started to throw them around the
living room, looking at Claud out of the
corner of her eye.

"No, no, little baby," said Claud. "Baby
shouldn't throw toys."

"Waaa!" cried Jenny. Then, as quickly as
she'd become a baby, she became a little girl
again. "I'm tired of this game," she said.
"Let's play Shark Attack."

So Claud played Shark Attack with Jenny
until the shark's batteries wore down and he
stopped moving around the board. Then
she and Jenny played with Barbie dolls for a

while. They had finished with that and were about to start on a game of hide-and-seek when Claud looked at her watch.

"Oops!" she said. "It's eight-fifteen, and you're supposed to be in bed by eight-thirty. Time to brush your teeth and get ready for bed." As they marched up the stairs together, Claud was already thinking about what she'd do after Jenny was asleep. She knew the Prezziosos wouldn't be home until at least ten-thirty, so she thought she'd have time to finish her maths homework. For once she'd remembered to bring her school stuff with her.

Just as she was squeezing the toothpaste onto Jenny's brush, Claud heard a funny noise downstairs. She tensed up. Jessi had told us about the report she'd heard on the radio, and I think we were all a bit nervous about burglars. Claud's an experienced enough sitter to be able to control her fears, though, so she hadn't thought much about thieves that night. And of course she'd made sure the doors were locked after the Prezziosos left.

But now she stopped what she was doing and listened closely. The noise had stopped. She handed Jenny's toothbrush to her, then stood by the bathroom door to listen some more. She heard the noise again! It sounded exactly like the door opening downstairs. "Oh, my lord," Claudia muttered.

"Whzzt?" asked Jenny, her mouth full of toothpaste.

"Nothing," said Claud. "Keep on brushing. You're doing a good job." As soon as Jenny turned back to the mirror, Claudia tiptoed into the hall.

"Claudia?" someone called from downstairs.

Claudia told me later that she nearly jumped through the ceiling. But she pulled herself together fast. "Mrs Prezzioso!" she said. "What are you doing home so early?"

Mr and Mrs Prezzioso were climbing the stairs together. "Why don't you put Jenny to bed," Mrs P. said to her husband. "I'll talk to Claudia." She led Claudia into the bedroom and motioned for her to sit on the bed. "Don't worry. Everything's all right," said Mrs P. She must have noticed the look on Claud's face.

"What happened?" asked Claudia.

"Well, we were at this dinner party," said Mrs P., "and another couple, the Gardellas, were there, too."

Claud drew in a breath. "I can ex—" she started.

"It's okay," said Mrs P. "We didn't believe what they were telling us. We've hired you girls as sitters for so long that we think we know you pretty well. And we know that none of you would ever steal from a client."

98

Claudia let out the breath she'd taken. "But why did you come home?" she asked.

"Well, we were kind of upset by what the Gardellas were saying. It turned the evening sour for us. I didn't want to have an argument with them, so we just left," said Mrs P.

Claud was impressed. "Wow," she said. "You really believe in us."

"Of course I do," said Mrs P. "Besides," she added in a lower voice, "between you and me, the party was a real bore. I didn't mind leaving."

Claud laughed. "Thanks for your support," she said. "But even if the party was no fun, I'm sorry you had to leave. You were looking forward to your night out."

"I know," said Mrs P. "But we'll go out again soon." She rummaged in her purse. "Here's pay for two hours' work," she said. "I'm sorry I can't pay you for the whole time."

Claud was sorry, too. She'd been counting on that money. But, as she told me later, what could she say? Mrs P. was being so nice. She left their house feeling pretty good, but by the time Mr P. had driven her home, Claudia had had more time to think and she was fuming. How could the Gardellas *do* that? How could they spread rumours about the club? It just wasn't fair.

12th CHAPTER

On that same Saturday night, while Claud was babysitting, I was at home with my mum. In a way I was glad I didn't have a sitting job that night. Ever since Mum had started working again, I don't get to spend too much time with her, and I miss her. We've got pretty close since the divorce (even though we still argue occasionally, as you know), and I honestly like just hanging out with her.

We'd made dinner together, after deciding that we both felt like spaghetti. I threw together a salad while she made a quick tomato sauce. Then we brought all the stuff to the table. It looked great, and I was starving. I helped myself to a big plate of spaghetti and sprinkled cheese all over it.

"So, no sitting job tonight?" asked my mum.

"No, no sitting job tonight, or tomorrow

night, or any other night this week," I answered glumly. Suddenly my spaghetti didn't look so good.

"Oh, Stacey," said my mum. "I'm sorry. Listen, I'm sure it's just a coincidence that business is slow. Your club has so many loyal clients. I know they wouldn't desert you."

"You're probably right," I said. But I'm sure I didn't sound too convinced—because I wasn't. Mum changed the subject, trying to distract me. She talked about the weather. She discussed the news of the day. She explained why she had decided to stop buying white bread. She told me about her job. But if she'd given me a test the next day on everything she'd said, I'm sorry to say I would have failed it. I just wasn't listening very well. I know that isn't nice, but I couldn't help it. My mind was on other things.

After dinner, I cleared the table and washed the dishes, without even being asked. After all, I thought, I had nothing better to do. I was almost finished when my mum walked into the kitchen. I must have looked pretty depressed, because she gave me a big hug.

"Come on, darling, cheer up!" she said. "Listen, how about if we rent a video and watch it together?"

"Okay," I said. "Why not?"

We drove to the video shop and spent

what seemed like *hours* picking out something. Everything I wanted to see she had no interest in, and vice versa. "How about this?" I asked, holding up a horror film about some girls at summer camp. I'd heard it was really good.

"Ugh!" said Mum. "I don't know how you can watch that junk. Now this," she said, holding up another video, "is a *real* film. *Holiday*, starring Cary Grant and Katharine Hepburn. Oh, isn't Cary Grant handsome! Don't you think?" She showed me the picture.

"I suppose so," I said, although I couldn't really see what was so great about him. "But don't tell me that film's in black and white. No way!"

She put the box back. We both kept looking. "How about this?" I asked. I'd found a concert film featuring my favourite group.

Mum shook her head. "I don't even like their records. I don't think I could stand watching them for two hours." She held up the box she'd been looking at. "This one is a classic."

"*It's a Wonderful Life*?" I said. "I can't say I agree with *that* these days. And anyway, I just don't feel like watching a 'classic'."

But then I found a classic I love—a film I could watch over and over again. And it's even in colour. "What do you say, Mum?" I asked, holding up the box. She gave me the thumbs-up sign, so I brought the box to the counter. *Gone With the Wind*. I think we've seen it about ten times, but we still love it. It's one film we can always agree to watch together.

We drove home, and while Mum went into the kitchen to make popcorn, I went upstairs to check my blood sugar and give myself some insulin.

Then we settled down to watch the film. By then I was feeling better about things. The popcorn was great, and as soon as I heard that *Gone With the Wind* theme music I was in heaven. But ten minutes into the film, the phone rang. "I'll get it," I said.

"Should I stop the VCR?" Mum asked.

"Just for a minute," I answered, as I picked up the phone. "Hello?" I said.

It was Claudia, and she sounded upset. Quickly, she told me what had happened at the Prezziosos. "This has really got out of hand," she said. "It's one thing when we don't get a lot of jobs, but then when I finally *do* get a job, it ends after an hour and a half!"

I felt terrible. "Maybe business will pick up again next week," I said hopefully.

"Not if the Gardellas have their way, it won't," she said. "Listen, how about if I come round? It's still early. I'm sure my dad won't mind driving me there."

"Of course," I replied, "I'd love to see

my best friend." We always turn to each other in bad times. After I'd hung up, I asked my mum if she wouldn't mind watching the film by herself, since Claudia was coming over. I thought Claud and I would just sit in my room. Maybe talking about the situation would make her feel better.

Mum understood. "Sounds like Claudia needs a friend right now," she said. "I'll be fine with Rhett and Scarlett for company."

But when Claud arrived and we went upstairs, she didn't seem to want any comforting. In fact, she seemed pretty cool towards me, and she wasn't talking much.

"So tell me again," I said. "Exactly what did Mrs Prezzioso say when she came home?"

Claudia was roaming around my room, picking things up and putting them down. She didn't look at me when she answered my question. "She said Mrs Gardella seemed convinced that you had taken her ring, but that Mrs P. didn't believe her."

"Well, that's good," I said. "I mean, Mrs P. knows me pretty well. And anybody who knows me knows I wouldn't steal."

"Yeah, well ..." Claud drifted over to my dressing table.

"So did she say anything else?" I asked.

"Just that the party was ruined for her and she didn't want to stay." Now Claud was looking through my make-up, moving

104

around my bottles and brushes and compacts.

"Do you want to try some of that new blusher I bought?" I asked. "It's really a good colour for me. I wonder whether it would work on you, too."

"What? Oh, no," said Claud. She seemed distracted, as if she were somewhere else.

"Claud," I said. "What's the matter?"

"Nothing's the matter," she answered. "Nothing at all." But she sounded really tense. I was beginning to feel that something weird was happening between us.

I tried to ignore it. "So what did Mrs P. wear to the party?" I asked. "She always looks as if she's stepped out of a magazine."

"I don't really remember," replied Claud.

Something was *definitely* up. Claud always pays a lot of attention to clothes. She can remember every outfit she's worn to school over a whole season, and she tries never to repeat the exact same outfit.

I looked closely at what Claudia was doing. She had finished checking out my make-up, and had started to look through my jewellery. I heard the tinkle of my musical jewellery box as she opened its lid. Then I watched as she started to look through my things. I couldn't work out what she was up to. She's seen my stuff a million times before. In fact, she's borrowed most of it once or twice. We're always swapping jewellery. But Claud looked serious this time as she checked each one of the little drawers and pulled out necklaces, earrings, and rings.

Rings.

All of a sudden I realized what she was doing. She was looking for Mrs Gardella's diamond ring! Even *Claudia*, my best friend, had become suspicious of me. I couldn't believe it.

"Claud, I know what you're doing," I said. My stomach was in a knot. "You're looking for that ring, aren't you?"

Claudia didn't answer straight away, but at least she took her hand out of the box for a moment. Then she drew in a deep breath. "Well, I am looking for it," she admitted. "I started to think on my way over here. You know, you did talk a lot about wanting a diamond ring. And now one is missing. I was wondering if this really was such a coincidence, after all."

"How *could* you?" I cried. "I thought you were my best friend." I felt as if I might start to cry any minute, but I fought back my tears.

"I just thought that before this went any further, I'd better make sure you really didn't have the ring," said Claudia.

"And?" I asked. "*Are* you sure, now that you've gone through all my private belongings?" I felt less like crying then. I was starting to get angry.

"I'm sure. "At least, I'm *pretty* sure."

That did it. "I can't believe you don't trust me," I said. "Anyway, if I did take the stupid ring, do you think I'd keep it in my jewellery box, where any fool could find it?"

Claudia just stared at me.

Oh, great, I thought. That was brilliant. Now I sounded as if I *had* taken the ring. "Look, search my whole room if you want," I said. "I don't care."

"I don't want to search your room," said Claud. "In fact, I don't even want to *be* in your room any more."

"Well, that's good," I said. "Because I'm kicking you out."

"Don't bother kicking me out," she said. "I'm leaving." She left without another look at me, slamming the door behind her. I opened it right away. I heard her run downstairs to the phone in the kitchen. I heard her call her father and ask him to pick her up. And then I heard her say something to my mother, and march through the front door to wait outside.

Some best friend, huh?

13th CHAPTER

I *hate* it when Claud and I row. I really do. We don't argue that often, but every time we do, it's just awful. The world can be a very lonely place when you and your best friend aren't speaking to each other.

All day Sunday, I thought of phoning Claudia. I wanted to make up with her. But you know what? As much as I wanted to make up, I did *not* want to apologize. I thought she was the one who owed me an apology. After all, best friends are supposed to trust each other, right?

So I sat round and waited for her to come to her senses and phone *me*. "Stacey?" she'd say. "I'm really sorry. I don't know what came over me. Of course you didn't steal that ring. Can you ever forgive me for doubting you?"

But the phone never rang. Well, that's not entirely true. It rang three times. Once someone from the subscription department of the local newspaper phoned, wanting to know if we would like to subscribe. Another call was from my dad. He wanted to find out when I was planning to visit him next. And the third call was a wrong number.

In between calls, I spent the weekend hanging round in my room: doing homework, reading magazines, listening to my Walkman, and thinking. After a weekend like that, it was almost a relief to go back to school on Monday.

Claudia avoided me in the corridors that day. I know she saw me, because I saw her. But we didn't make eye contact, and we didn't say hello. I skipped lunch in the cafeteria and went to the library instead. I sat at one of the corner tables and ate my sandwich and apple quietly, so the librarian wouldn't kick me out for eating in there.

I was feeling pretty lonely.

But I was also feeling kind of good. I had decided that something had to be done about the situation with the Gardellas, and I thought I might have come up with a solution to the problem. It wasn't a perfect solution, but it was something. I would tell everybody about it at the club meeting this afternoon. If they liked my idea, I'd go ahead with it.

I was careful not to get to the meeting too early that day; I did *not* want to be alone with Claudia. When I *did* get there, I felt funny walking up the stairs to her room. I've walked up those stairs so many times, and just about every other time I've been looking forward to seeing my best friend. But that day I was dreading it.

I was relieved when I walked into club headquarters and saw Kristy, Dawn, and Jessi already there. They looked up and said hello when I walked in, but Claud ignored my entrance.

She was sitting on the bed next to Dawn, so no way was I going to sit on the bed, too. I didn't really want to sit in my other usual spot—the desk chair—because then I'd be facing Claud. I decided to sit on the floor near Jessi, with my back against the bed. That way I wouldn't have to look at Claudia *or* be near her.

I don't know if everybody was talking before I arrived, but they certainly weren't saying anything once I'd sat down. The room was very quiet. I could hear a rustle as Claudia opened a bag of Hula Hoops. (Of course, I wasn't looking at her, so I wasn't *positive* they were Hula Hoops; they might have been Tortilla chips or Crinkle-cuts. But my guess is that they were Hula Hoops because those are favourites of Claud's.)

After a couple of minutes I heard footsteps on the stairs and then Mary Anne and Mallory came into the room. Mary Anne gave me a funny look when she saw where I was sitting, but then she shrugged and took a seat on the bed. Mal sat on the floor next to Jessi, and smiled at me.

"Okay," said Kristy. "We're all here and it's five-thirty. Let's get started." She leaned back in the director's chair and straightened her visor. "Does anybody have any club business?"

Somehow I wasn't ready yet to tell them my idea. But there was something else I had to do. "Well, it's Monday," I said. "Subs day."

Everybody groaned.

"You know," said Claudia. "I don't think we should have to *pay* subs when we're not earning any money."

"But we always pay subs!" said Mary Anne. She sounded shocked.

"That's right," agreed Kristy. "We need that money in our treasury, no matter how slow business is."

"It was just a thought," said Claudia crossly.

Now I *really* didn't want to look at her. I pulled out the manila envelope that we use for a treasury and held it behind me, waiting for someone on the bed to take it from me so I wouldn't have to turn around.

"Okay," said Kristy, once the envelope had made its rounds. "Now listen. We've all heard about what happened with the Prezziosos on Saturday, right?"

Oh, great. If Claud had told everybody *that* story, then she must have also told them about our argument. Did they feel the same way she did? Did they suspect me, too? It didn't seem like it. At least the others were speaking to me and acting more or less like my friends. So even if Claud had told them, maybe they hadn't made up their minds who to side with.

"Yeah," said Jessi, answering Kristy's question. "And I can't believe the nerve of those Gardellas."

"What they're doing isn't right," said Mallory.

"It's not," agreed Mary Anne. "But they *are* doing it. And we've got to work out how to deal with it."

"Right. Before our reputation is completely ruined," said Dawn. "This club could go out of business if we don't do something."

"But what can we do?" asked Claud. "I mean, they're adults, and we're just kids. We can't go around telling everybody that the Gardellas are liars."

"No," said Kristy. "But they're not exactly liars, anyway. They really think Stacey took that ring."

"And they think our clients have a right to know," said Mal. "What a mess."

"Well," I said, realizing that it was now or never. I cleared my throat. "I've got an idea," I paused.

"Well, go on!" said Kristy. "We need all the ideas we can get."

"I was thinking," I said. "I know something has to be done, and I think I'm the one to do it. I hope my plan will save the club—and maybe it will also help me prove I'm not an awful person and a thief."

"We know you're not, Stacey," said Mary Anne.

"Well, most of us do, anyway," I said. "I know I shouldn't feel like I have to prove myself to my *friends*. . . ." I could feel Claudia looking at the back of my head. I hoped she felt bad about what she'd done.

"So what's your plan?" asked Kristy.

I took a deep breath. "I thought I would offer to babysit for free for the Gardellas, until the price of the ring is paid off."

Everybody was quiet for a moment. Then Jessi spoke up. "Wow," she said, quietly. "But you didn't take the ring."

"I know," I said. "And I know I shouldn't have to pay them back for it. I don't even know what they'll think when I tell them my plan. Will they think I'm proving I'm innocent—or just admitting I'm guilty?"

"Whatever they think, *I* think it's a good plan," said Kristy. "It'll clean up your record with them, and then the club can start fresh. Anyway, it's the best idea we've heard yet. I think you should go for it."

Everybody else seemed to agree, too, so I decided to phone Mrs Gardella straightaway. I dialled her number and when she answered I told her who it was. She sounded a little surprised.

"Why, Stacey," she said. "I didn't expect to hear from you."

"I know," I said. "But I was hoping I could clear things up between us." Mrs Gardella didn't say anything, so I plunged ahead. "I was wondering if you would let me babysit for free for you until I've paid off whatever the ring cost."

She was quiet for a moment, which made me nervous. Then she said, "Well, that's very generous of you, considering that you insist that you didn't take the ring."

"I didn't," I said. "But somehow I feel responsible for the fact that it's missing. Anyway, maybe if you let me have another chance to sit for you you'll learn to trust me again."

There was another long pause on the other end of the line. I raised my eyebrows at Kristy while I waited for Mrs Gardella to make up her mind. Finally, she said, "I suppose it's only fair to give you a chance to make things right. But I'm afraid I just don't feel comfortable leaving you alone in the house. I'll agree to your offer, but only if someone else from your club comes with you, at least the first time."

"Uh, well, okay. How about the club chairman, Kristy Thomas?" I asked, raising my eyebrows at Kristy again.

114

"That would be fine," said Mrs Gardella. "Would you like to start this Friday?"

"Fine," I said. "Let me check with Kristy." I put my hand over the mouth-piece of the phone and whispered to Kristy. "She says it's okay but she doesn't want me to come alone. Would you come with me? This Friday?"

Kristy nodded. "Seems kind of weird to me," she said. "But if it'll save the club, I'll do it."

I took my hand off the mouthpiece. "That's fine," I said to Mrs Gardella. "What time would you like us to be there?"

She asked us to come at eight-thirty. She still sounded a bit hesitant, but I suppose she realized how badly I wanted the chance to prove myself.

I hung up once we'd agreed on the details, and gave a big sigh. "Wow," I said. "This is really getting complicated."

"Yeah," said Mallory. "And do you realize that we *still* don't know what really did happen to the ring?"

I smiled at her. I was glad she trusted me.

"Do you think it really could have been taken by the burglar?" asked Jessi, her eyes round. So she believed me, too. Not *everybody* was a traitor, like my supposed best friend.

We spent the rest of the meeting trying to work out what could have happened to the ring. Mary Anne wondered if the baby might have swallowed it. Dawn thought Mrs Gardella might have dropped it down the drain without noticing. Jessi seemed convinced that it was the burglar. And Kristy thought that it had just been misplaced and the Gardellas hadn't looked very hard for it.

The only person who didn't offer a theory was Claud. But I knew what *she* thought, and I was just glad she didn't speak up.

The meeting passed quickly—so fast, in fact, that I was surprised when I heard Kristy say, "Okay, that's it for today!"

The phone hadn't rung once. We all realized it at the same moment.

"Oh well," said Dawn. "There *is* a bright side to all of this. At least if we're not going on jobs, we don't have to write in the club notebook!"

Kristy threw a pillow at her, but the rest of us cracked up. It was nice to know we could still find something to laugh at.

14th CHAPTER

On Friday, Kristy came to my house for supper after our meeting. Then my mum drove us to the Gardellas'. I felt a little down, because (if my plan worked) I'd be sitting for free for a long, long time. Even so, I was determined to do my best, because it was the only solution I could see to my—and the club's—problem.

As we stood on the Gardellas' front porch, ringing the bell, I looked over at Kristy. I was suddenly really, really happy that she was there with me. "Thanks," I said, hoping she'd know what I meant.

"No problem," she answered. "I just hope I don't have to come with you *every* time!" We laughed.

Mrs Gardella answered the door, and I was relieved to see that she was acting normally. Normal for Mrs Gardella, that is. After I'd introduced Kristy to her, she gave

117

us the same house tour that she'd given me the first time I'd been there. She kept going on about how Bird had had an upset stomach lately, and explaining that we were to feed him only a bit of food at a time. Mouse was feeling fine, but he hadn't had much attention that day, so she wanted us to be sure to play with him once Tara was asleep.

"And Tara here," she said, boosting the baby up to her shoulder, "will need a bottle soon, and then she'll be ready for bed."

We nodded.

"I hope this works out for us, Stacey," Mrs Gardella said, looking at me. "Even when our nanny comes back, it would be nice to have a back-up sitter. We'd like to be able to trust you to be that person."

At first I didn't know what to say. "I hope so, too," I said finally.

As soon as the door closed behind Mr and Mrs Gardella, Kristy looked at me in amazement. "Can you believe them?" she asked. "They treat their animals as if they were people!"

"I know. They're something else. But isn't Tara cute?"

Kristy leaned towards Tara, who was sitting on the sofa between us. "You *are* cute," she said, letting Tara grab onto her finger. "You are about the cutest baby I've ever seen. And you can't help it that your parents are lunatics!"

118

"Kristy!" I said. I couldn't believe she said that.

"What?" Kristy replied. "Tara can't understand a word I'm saying. And I was only kidding, anyway. But speaking of lunatics, did you hear that report on the radio last night? The police still haven't caught the burglar."

"I know," I said. "That makes me nervous. Let's make sure all the doors are locked." I'd never thought much of Jessi's theory that the burglar was the one who took Mrs Gardella's ring, but now the idea sent a shiver down my spine. Suppose he *had* been in the house with me that night?

Kristy checked the front door. "It's locked," she said. "And I'll put the chain on, too—just in case."

I made sure the windows were locked. Then we checked the back door and the basement door. "Do you think we should look around upstairs?" I asked. "I mean, to make sure the burglar isn't under a bed or something?"

"Oh, Stacey," said Kristy. "Don't be silly. Burglars don't hide under beds." Then she glanced at me. I must have looked scared. "Okay," she said. "If it'll make you feel better."

We trooped upstairs (I was carrying Tara) and checked inside each cupboard and under every bed, including Tara's cot. Ordinarily, neither of us would ever go round looking in our clients' cupboards. We *never* snoop. But these were not normal circumstances. Mouse and Bird followed us from room to room, sniffing each place as if they were also checking for burglars.

"Okay?" Kristy asked. "I think we're the only people in the house, don't you?"

"Yup," I said. "Nobody here but us chickens." That's from an old joke my dad taught me when I was little—about a thief in a hen coop who says that line when the farmer yells, "Who's in there?"

Kristy laughed. I suppose she'd heard the joke from Watson. Then she said, "Can I give Tara her bottle? I haven't taken care of a baby for ages, and I miss it."

"Okay," I answered. We headed for the kitchen and warmed up the bottle. When it was ready, Kristy sat on the sofa with Tara, feeding her. I watched quietly. Tara's eyelids were drooping, and I knew that if we didn't startle her she'd fall asleep easily.

Sure enough, by the time the bottle was half empty, Tara was practically asleep. Kristy lifted her to her shoulder and burped her, then carried her carefully upstairs. I followed—and Mouse and Bird followed *me*. The minute Tara was in her cot, she started to breathe deeply.

"Out like a light," said Kristy. "What an easy baby to sit for!"

"*She's* easy," I said. "But these two are another story." I pointed at Mouse and Bird who were looking hopefully at us. "I suppose they know it's dinnertime," I said.

Kristy turned out the light in Tara's room and we went downstairs. Preparing dinner for the animals took longer than getting Tara's bottle warmed, but finally everything was ready. I put out just a little bit for Bird, but he ate it right up so I gave him seconds. Mouse wolfed down *his* dinner before I could even turn round.

After the animals had eaten, we all went into the living room. Bird curled up underneath the coffee table (one of his favouirite spots, according to Mrs Gardella), but Mouse seemed to want to play. He batted at our ankles when we tried to talk, demanding attention. There were some cat toys in a small basket next to the sofa, and I pulled one out.

"A mouse for a Mouse," I said, throwing it down near him. He jumped on the little stuffed mouse immediately, grabbing it in his mouth and shaking it back and forth.

"What's he *doing*?" I asked.

"Um, he's killing it," said Kristy. "If it were a real mouse, that would break its neck. I saw Boo-Boo do it once."

"Oh, ugh!" I said. "That's disgusting." Just then, Mouse took the toy in his mouth, got up, and walked out of the room. A couple of minutes later, just as Kristy and I were starting to talk about this new substitute teacher we both have, he came back in. Without the toy.

"Did you lose it?" I asked. "Well, here's another." I reached into the basket and threw him a tiny little pillow that must have been full of catnip. He went crazy! He rolled all over it, and then batted it around the room. His eyes were shining so that he looked like a little tiger. Kristy thought it was really funny, but I was worried. What if he was sick from the catnip? The Gardellas would never forgive me.

I was about to take the toy away from Mouse when he got up, took the pillow in his mouth, and walked out of the room. And then, once again, he returned without it.

We kept giving him toys: little balls with bells inside them, a miniature cat with a long tail for him to chase, and another stuffed mouse. He played with them all, but then he carried one out of the room and came back without it.

"What does he *do* with all of them?" asked Kristy.

"I don't know," I said. "But I'm going to find out." When he came back the next time, I gave him a little stuffed bird. Sure enough, after he'd played with it for a while, he picked it up in his mouth and walked off. I got up and followed him, hoping he wouldn't notice. He didn't even look over his shoulder.

Mouse headed for a desk in the Gardellas' library. He stopped in front of it, put the bird down on the rug, and then gently batted it with his paw until it rolled under the desk.

"Aha!" I said. "So this is your hiding place." I got down on my hands and knees to see what was under there. I saw the bird, the two mice, some foil balls, the ball with the bells, and the miniature cat.

"I'll get those for you," I said to Mouse. "We're almost out of toys, anyway. We need these back." I rummaged around in a cupboard until I found a broom. Then I bent down again and used it to sweep the toys out from under the desk.

"There you go," I said. (I couldn't believe I was talking to this cat like he was a person. It must have been the Gardellas' influence.) But Mouse was nowhere to be seen. "Mouse," I called. "Where are you?"

"He's in here," called Kristy from the living room. "He got tired of waiting for you, so he found some other toys on his own."

I came in to look. Mouse had found a pile of plastic twist-ties, the kind used to tie up plastic bags, and he seemed to be in heaven. He would toss one of them in the air, and then he'd go crazy chasing it around when it landed.

Then he started to pick *those* up and carry them away. Only this time he wasn't going to the library. This time he was heading for the TV room. I was curious, so I followed him on his next trip.

Mouse headed for the corner of the rug that was under the TV. He put down the twist-tie and batted it underneath the rug where there was a little wrinkle. "You crazy cat," I said. "You've got hiding places all over this house, haven't you?"

I walked over and lifted up the rug. Sure enough, a whole pile of twist-ties was there, plus a lot of paper clips, plus . . . *a diamond ring*! I gasped and put my hand over my mouth. "Oh, my lord," I said to myself. Then I yelled for Kristy.

She couldn't believe it. "The ring was here all along!" she said. "This is incredible."

"What should we do?" I asked.

"Let's leave everything just as it is," she said. "That way we can show it to the Gardellas when they come home."

I have to admit that I felt pretty smug as I led Mr and Mrs Gardella into the TV room later that night. And when I pulled back the rug, and heard Mrs Gardella gasp, I felt even better. Now she knew I wasn't a thief.

"Oh, Stacey," she said. "I am *so* sorry. I can't believe I didn't think to check Mouse's hiding places. You wouldn't believe how many little things we've lost this way. But this is a new hiding place. I didn't even know about it."

I explained how I'd followed Mouse around to see what he was doing.

"That was clever," said Mrs Gardella. "I really don't know how to apologize to you. I feel terrible. First thing in the morning I'll phone the Prezziosos and tell them they were right to stand up for you."

"Oh, thanks," I said. "Um, do you think you could call everyone else, too?"

"Everybody else?" she repeated. "We didn't tell anyone else. I've been so busy, with Bird sick and all."

I was surprised. Maybe it *had* just been a coincidence that we'd received so few job calls lately.

"Well, anyway, I'm glad you've got your ring back," I said.

Mr Gardella drove me and Kristy home. And when he paid us, I noticed that he gave us about double what we should have earned. I suppose he felt as bad as his wife did.

15th CHAPTER

"Okay, everybody," I said. "Cough up!" I passed round the manila envelope. It was subs day again. The Babysitters Club was back to business as usual.

I smiled at Claudia as she emptied out her penny jar and started to count. "Down to the last few cents, huh?" I asked. "Don't worry. You'll be rich again soon."

Claudia smiled back. "I can't believe we've already got five jobs arranged for this week. Clients hardly ever call my number except during club meetings, but this week the phone has been ringing off the hook." She shook her head over the pile of pennies she'd made. "Now I've lost count," she said, starting again.

Boy, did it feel good to be friends with Claud again. We'd made up over the weekend. In fact, she had called me, planning to apologize, while I was still at the

Gardellas'. So she had realized she was wrong even *before* I'd been proved innocent. That made me feel terrific. Claudia and I had spent Saturday at the arcade just window-shopping, since neither of us had any money. And Sunday was rainy, so we spent the day in her room, trying out new hairstyles.

"So what did Mrs Perkins say when she phoned?" asked Kristy. Claudia had already told us about the calls she'd got, but we needed to hear the details.

"She said they had been on holiday, and she and her husband had really enjoyed spending time with the girls, but now they were back and she was ready to line up some sitters again," said Claudia. The Perkinses have two little girls—Gabbie and Myriah—and a baby named Laura.

"And what did Dr Johanssen say?" asked Mary Anne.

Claudia laughed. "I already told you this," she said, "but okay. Charlotte had flu and she didn't want to expose us to it. But Charlotte's fine now. And Stacey, you've got a job with her on Wednesday."

"Great!" I said. Charlotte's one of my favourite kids to sit for. She's almost like a little sister to me.

Claudia finished telling us about the rest of the calls she'd received. The Newtons. The Addisons. The Braddocks. They all had very good reasons for not phoning us recently, and they all needed sitters again. Our reputation was as good as ever. What a relief!

Mary Anne was going over the club record book. "Wow, we're going to be busy for the next couple of weeks," she said. "We may have to call on Shannon and Logan to help us if we get too many more jobs."

Just then the phone rang. Kristy answered it. "Oh, hello, Mrs Gardella," she said, making a face at me. "Yes, we're glad, too. Oh, really? Well, that's nice. Thanks for letting us know. 'Bye!"

Kristy hung up. "She said she was 'so glad the mess had been cleared up,' and she was sorry—for the fortieth time." Kristy smiled at me. "She also said their nanny is back so she won't need us much any more."

"Good!" I said. "You know what? I wasn't going to sit for them again, anyway. We don't need clients like that, when we've got all our good old regulars back."

"I agree with Stacey," said Mary Anne shyly. "I don't think we should sit for people who don't trust us and who would spread rumours about us."

Everybody nodded. "It's unanimous," said Kristy. "We won't sit for the Gardellas again, even if their nanny deserts them. We don't need business that badly."

"It's quite sad, though," I said thoughtfully. "Tara is the sweetest baby."

"But what about Mouse and Bird?"

asked Kristy. "I mean, we're *baby*sitters, not spoiled-animal-sitters."

We all laughed. Then the phone rang again. It was Mrs Barrett, looking for a sitter for Buddy, Suzi, and Marnie.

"They were away on holiday," said Kristy after she'd hung up. "That's why she hasn't called lately. But she says Buddy misses Mallory, and he asked for her especially. The job's on Saturday afternoon."

Mary Anne was looking at the record book. She gasped and put her hand over her mouth. "Oh!" she said. "That's right. I have a little note here saying 'Barretts to Grand Canyon.' I forgot all about their holiday." She shook her head. "Well, I'm glad they're back. And yes, Mallory is free, but so are you, Stacey," she said.

"You take the job," I said to Mal. "I've already got two others lined up."

The phone rang throughout the meeting —just like the old days. One of the last calls was from Jessi's mum, Mrs Ramsey. She wanted to remind Jessi that she and Mr Ramsey had tickets to the theatre that Saturday, and that Aunt Cecelia would be away visiting cousins.

"I remembered," said Jessi, when the call was over. "And I'm looking forward to the job. At least I don't have to worry about that old burglar any more."

"What?" asked Mary Anne. "Did he get caught?"

"Didn't you hear?" asked Jessi. "It was on the radio last night. I think he wasn't the most brilliant burglar in the world. They caught him because he left his wallet at one of the houses he robbed. And get this," she went on. "The wallet was under a sofa, but the family's dog pulled it out when they were sitting around watching TV!"

"I don't believe it," I said. "That's incredible! That dog must have been taking lessons from Mouse."

"And once the police had his wallet, it wasn't too hard to find him," added Claudia. "His driver's licence was in there, along with all kinds of other ID."

"Well," said Jessi. "I am so, so glad he got caught. I was scared he'd turn up while I was babysitting somewhere."

"Do you know what to do if a burglar *does* turn up?" asked Kristy. "It's important to know how to deal with a situation like that."

"Umm," said Jessi. "I suppose I'd try to get the kids out of the house without attracting his attention."

"Good!" said Kristy. "That would be common sense."

"I'd never try to stop a burglar myself," added Mary Anne.

"Nobody should," said Kristy. "It's best just to try to get out of his way."

"But what about the police?" asked Mal.

"You could call them from a neighbour's house," I suggested.

"Right," said Kristy. "Get the children out of the house first, then work out how to let the police know what's happening. The main thing is to make sure the kids are safe."

"I still hope it never happens to me," said Jessi. "I'm not sure if I could handle it without panicking."

"Of course you could," said Mal loyally. "You're not the panicky type. I'm sure you'd be fine."

"I suppose so," said Jessi. "I did manage to hide how scared I was that time with Becca and Squirt, so at least I know I can do that. But if I really saw a burglar—"

"Well, it'll probably never happen anyway," said Kristy. "But it's good to be prepared."

"Enough about burglars," said Dawn. "I have a proposal to make. I think we deserve a healthy pizza party, and I'm inviting all of you over this Friday. How about it?"

"Yea!" everybody cried at once.

"Anyone who has a sitting job can come late," said Dawn. "We'll make it a sleepover."

"Is there enough money in the treasury for pizza?" asked Kristy.

I checked. "There certainly is," I replied. "Good thing we kept paying subs."

"Good thing," echoed Claudia, grinning at me. "By the way, Stacey, I want to give you something. I know it doesn't make up for what I did, and I know it's not exactly the jewellery you're dreaming of, but . . ."

She handed me a little box. I took it and opened it. "Oh, it's beautiful!" I said, holding up what she'd given me for everyone to see. "Did you make this?"

Claud nodded. "I'm glad you like it," she said.

I held it in my palm, looking at it. It was an earcuff (a *very* cool accessory these days) with a collection of blue stones and beads hanging from it. "I love it," I said. "Thanks, Claud." I passed the box around so everybody could take a look. "And by the way, I may get the birthstone ring after all," I said. "My mum told me last night that she and my dad talked about it, and they might club together to get it for me for my next birthday—or for Christmas, or some other special occasion."

"All right!" cried Claud.

"Wow," said Jessi and Mallory together.

"You're so lucky," added Mary Anne.

"Babysitters Club," said Kristy. She was answering the phone. It had rung one more time while we were talking. At the sound, we grinned at each other. It was good to be back in business.

True Horror Stories
by *Terry Deary*

A chilling collection of terrifying tales that each claim to be true, presented by Terry Deary in all their spine-chilling reality. But, is there a plausible explanation . . .?
A whole village of people disappears without trace, and all anyone saw were strange lights in the sky.
An Egyptian mummy, disturbed after thousands of years, leaves a trail of horrible disasters.
Consider the facts and decide for yourself whether each gruesome story really is true – but keep the cover firmly closed once darkness falls, or your dreams could turn into NIGHTMARES . . .

True Monster Stories
by *Terry Deary*

Incredible? Impossible? Too awful to imagine? But someone, somewhere at some time has sworn that each of these strange stories is true . . .
Read accounts of the Yeti, the vampire, and less well-known beasts, like Black Dog and Mogawr; consider the facts and decide for yourself whether these monster stories really are true. And even if you choose not to believe, beware! These tales may linger in your thoughts and darken your dreams . . .

LOOK IN TO THE FUN WORLD OF HIPPO ACTIVITY!

My Secret Picture Album
by *Tat Small* and *Steve Wetherill*

Hands Off My Picture Album!

A special secret book to fill with your favourite drawings, photos, cuttings and all sorts of souvenirs. With facts, jokes, games, puzzles and hints on how to take a fantastic photo.

My Secret Yearbook
by *Tat Small* illustrated by *Steve Weatherill*

Want to know who my best friend is? Who's in my secret club? Sorry, but this is MY book and it's private. So keep out!

My First Sticker Diary
by *Tat Small* illustrated by *Nick Sharratt*

A diary with a difference . . .

An exciting idea for a first diary. Each page follows an interesting theme, with lots of fill-in ideas. And, there's plenty of colourful stickers to fit each page!

The Lunchbox Book
by *Jennie Walters* illustrated by *Rowan Barnes-Murphy*

A book that looks so real, your mouth won't stop watering!

A book that looks like a lunchbox! It even has a press-out handle so you can carry it around with you! Inside there are some lovely ideas for lunchtime treats, plus quizzes, fun facts, and some juicy jokes too.

Twenty Spine-Tingling Mini Mysteries
by *Dino Anastasio* illustrated by *Kim Blundell*

Here are twenty chilling mysteries for you to solve. A bloody thumbprint, strange noises in the night and a mysterious hotel burglary . . . can you find an explanation for each of these sinister stories?